R. H. LEES

# A QUESTION OF MURDER

*Complete and Unabridged*

# LINFORD
*Leicester*

First published in Great Britain by
Robert Hale Limited, London

First Linford Edition
published 2006
by arrangement with
Robert Hale Limited, London

Apart from those historically recorded,
all incidents, locations and characters
are entirely imaginary.

British Library CIP Data

Lees, R. H.
    A question of murder.—Large print ed.—
Linford mystery library
    1. Detective and mystery stories
    2. Large type books
    I. Title
    823.9'14 [F]

    ISBN 1–84617–227–6

Published by
F. A. Thorpe (Publishing)
Anstey, Leicestershire

Set by Words & Graphics Ltd.
Anstey, Leicestershire
Printed and bound in Great Britain by
T. J. International Ltd., Padstow, Cornwall

This book is printed on acid-free paper

# A QUESTION OF MURDER

When Arthur Burnett died in the Rhodesian bush, Randall realised that Burnett was the one mentioned in the cryptogram. Inspector Sturman ridiculed Randall's suggestion that it could be foul play. So Randall proves that one of Burnett's African employees had been murdered and finds a mystic hill which only one African would dare to climb . . . Whilst observing animal behaviour, he comes upon a gruesome scene and almost loses his own life before solving the mystery.

# Prelude

The two Africans had left the village soon after dawn for it would take them several hours to reach the forest. If they were successful in their quest they might be back in time for the evening meal, but they were not committed — if need be they would spend the night there.

It was the beginning of summer — a summer that had arrived with a warmth not due for another month. The previous wet season had been a poor one — not a drought — but the rains had ended prematurely, causing the grass to dry out earlier than usual which would mean the cattle being in poor condition by the onset of the next rains. The men had known worse and were philosophical.

Today they were going to search for wild bees' nests, and hoping that any they found would have plenty of honey, each carried a gourd in which to bring back combs.

They reached the edge of the forest by midmorning and set about attracting a honey guide bird, which they trusted would lead them to a hive. Some bee larvae would be left for the bird of course, as was customary.

To attract a bird, the older native rapped a few times on a tree-trunk with his axe, repeating this ploy every few minutes as they made their way into the lightly wooded terrain.

After a while they heard the excited 'chur, chur, chur' of one of these birds and started to follow it amongst the trees, rapping regularly to encourage it. They had followed it for perhaps a mile when it began to fly back and forth between the branches of one particular tree, and looking carefully, the two men could see bees issuing from a hole in the trunk about ten feet from the ground.

The older man handed his axe to his companion. 'Continue tapping occasionally or the bird will be offended, thinking we are not going to open the hive. I will look for a small log to lean against the tree so that we can reach it,' he told him and strode off to find one.

Not finding anything suitable in the immediate vicinity he searched further afield. The stench of rotting flesh filled his nostrils indicating that some animal had died hereabouts. He spat in disgust, but from curiosity decided to find out what kind of animal it was. He saw something lying beneath a large shady tree and made towards it. Suddenly, rooted to the spot, he yelled for his companion to come.

The putrefying carcase was clothed. It was the body of a white man. A rifle lay nearby and an uncorked water-bottle was close to the man's hand.

They touched nothing, picked up their gourds and axe, and at a steady lope, set off for the village where they found the headman and told him of their gruesome find.

He immediately despatched a cyclist to the nearest police officer to report the news.

The village became alive with chattering. The headman shuddered. He had known something horrible would happen ever since the owl had settled on his hut and hooted.

# 1

For the second time, the 'remittance man' considered the auctioneer's notice.

Peter Carsten Randall was not a remittance man in the generally accepted sense, though technically no doubt he was, and he often described himself as such. A remittance man was usually the black sheep of a family and sent to the colonies to be out of the way, where he could no longer be an embarrassment.

Peter Randall had no such family to disgrace and though his remittance had come from a branch of it, it came from generosity and affection as distinct from bribery.

After losing both his parents at an early age he had entered the South African postal service in his teens where he had quickly become proficient in telegraphy. Unfortunately his handwriting was very poor and he had found it a considerable strain to write legibly at speed, so, when an uncle in England died, leaving him a small investment income, he had taken the opportunity to put that kind of work behind him.

When quite young, someone had once asked him what he would like to be. 'Retired' he had answered!

Now at the age of twenty-seven and having moved to Bulawayo, he had reached the stage, where, though not able to retire completely, he was at least able to live comfortably by augmenting his legacy income in several ways, all of which he enjoyed. He spent a few hours each week keeping a set of books for a small trader, wrote articles (mainly on natural history) for a periodical, and dealt in a little buying and selling of small articles, usually purchased at auctions, having a natural flair for this latter enterprise. He was very selective, dealing only in pieces of china, silverware, old books etc, which after cleaning or repairing he was able to sell at a profit, sometimes through Press advertisements or at another of the numerous auctions, for apart from the daytime disposals of estates on site, sales were held every Thursday night at the auctioneers' own halls.

Now as Randall studied the advertisement before him his eye kept returning to one item: 'Greener shotgun, slightly damaged.'

These expensive but high-quality guns usually fetched a good price. 'Slightly damaged' could mean a little or a lot and though guns did not usually interest him, if this were something he could get repaired cheaply there was a good chance of a few pounds profit.

He pondered too, on why, at a sale of household effects of a Miss Maidwell, there should be a shotgun and wondered if there might be other items of interest. He checked the time of the sale, 10.00 a.m. on the morrow, and made a note of the address, Acacia Avenue, Suburbs.

The expensive residential area to the east of the town was always referred to as the 'suburbs' although there were several other residential districts on the town's outskirts.

Next day, his car requiring some minor attention, he walked to the sale, leaving sufficiently early to allow ample time to examine any articles which might interest him, but soon realized that there were very few on this occasion. The lots were comprised almost entirely of household furniture, garden tools and implements. The shotgun had obviously received very rough treatment and having little knowledge of gun mechanism, he decided at once that it was not for him. There were however, several bundles of books displayed on the dining-room table.

As seems to be the custom at auctions, only one interesting book was placed in each bundle together with a number of old text-books or novels, thus ensuring that the buyer who wanted one particular item was compelled to take the rubbish also.

Now interested only in the books, Randall found himself having to wait nearly two hours before the auctioneer reached them. Few bidders were competing with him and in less than ten minutes he had secured the half dozen bundles.

Selecting a native youth from the number awaiting such commissions, he arranged for him to carry them back to his flat and himself set off for home, feeling quite excited about his purchase, for among a bundle containing books on *Electricity and Magnetism*, *The Principles of Telephony* and some cheap novels, he had noticed a copy of Metterlink's *A Dissertation on the Myths and Mysteries of Central and Southern Africa*, which had been published at the turn of the century.

Though not yet classified as a rarity it was sufficiently uncommon to be sought after and would certainly turn out to be a sound investment.

He greatly looked forward to reading it as the author was known to have delved deeply into the subject and to have personally researched into all the questions raised.

★  ★  ★

As a bachelor, it was his custom to take his evening meal at a restaurant in the town — a meal lasting perhaps an hour and a half, as he usually met others similarly placed, and together they would discuss the topics of the day.

That night however he was keen to examine his purchase and making some excuse, returned home somewhat earlier than he normally did, donned his slippers, put a glass and a bottle of whisky close to his easy chair and prepared for a pleasant evening. Not that he was by any means a heavy drinker — a single 'sun-downer' before leaving for the restaurant was his daily quota, but this evening he intended to enjoy himself.

Opening the book he found that apart from a single map depicting the territory covered by the work, and where significant, the pinpointing of specific places, the only other illustration was the frontispiece — a photograph of the author — a massive man, heavily whiskered and bearded. On the flyleaf, written in a clear and flowing hand was the message, 'Laurie. Knew this book would interest you. Warmest regards. Allen.' On the opposite page and apparently written by the recipient was inscribed:

L. Maidwell
Postmaster
Banshabi.

So, Maidwell had been a postmaster. That explained the number of technical books he had had to take in the bundles.

The opening chapters covered the more or less well-known mythical animals — the East African Nandi Bear, reputedly seen on more occasions than was ever the Abominable Snowman, yet still without any actual specimen ever having been obtained, though the spoor has been traced and casts taken, the generally accepted explanation being that it was a huge hyena.

The Sandhlawana, another animal no one seems to have been able to photograph or to have seen dead, yet the hairs of the animal (the possession of which are reputed to bring good luck), are sold for as much as a pound a hair and still find gullible buyers! The case of the 'Talking Baboon'. This one pure fantasy. The 'Baboon Boy'. Quite genuine, being an African child brought up in a baboon pack.

A complete chapter on the 'Tokoloshi', a mischievous spirit believed in implicitly by all Africans and blamed for all unexplained household mishaps.

He read on, coming now to chapters on lost gold strikes, and the finds in some of the old ruins by the 'Ancient Ruins Exploration Co.' who were reported to have taken hundreds of ounces of gold trinkets from such places as Zimbabwe, Dhlo Dhlo and Khami ruins. Metterlink discoursed on the probable likelihood of the connection between Southern Rhodesia and the Biblical 'Land of Ophir' and 'King Solomon's Mines'.

Towards midnight the final page was reached. As he was about to close the volume and help himself to the drink which until then he had completely forgotten, two lines penned on the opposite flyleaf caught his eye.

S 5 5 P I G 5 N D 1 R O H 2 R
7 2 R 9 5 0 0 K 9 T W S

While he slowly sipped his drink he pondered on the apparent cryptogram but could make nothing of it. Tomorrow would be another day. He would look at it again then.

# 2

The following morning, it being Friday, Randall put in his weekly appearance at the two-man company of Gleeman and Klein, manufacturers' representatives, this being the firm whose accounts he kept. Klein he had never met, and Gleeman seemed to be out more often than in, doing his own 'Rep.' duties. Though efficient and progressive in doing business, keeping records was quite another matter and in consequence Randall found handling the accounts quite a challenge — but one he enjoyed. Normally he would expect to complete his work by about noon and being already in town, would have his lunch at the restaurant.

This day however, having been faced with a particularly obscure discrepancy he had been unable to leave the office until after one o'clock and finding the restaurant crowded as he had anticipated, he settled for a packet of sandwiches and made his way home. A copy of his home-town newspaper had arrived by post that morning and he looked forward to perusing it over his meal.

He turned the pages for some fifteen minutes but finding less in it than usual to interest him, he soon put it aside and picked up the *Dissertation*, having only then remembered the enigmatic inscription on the end flyleaf. What could be the meaning of it? Hardly the handiwork of a child — the calligraphy was too clear and precise. It appeared to have been written at the same time as the inscription to 'Laurie' on the front flyleaf, for the ink was obviously the same, and although penned in block letters there was a distinct similarity.

It seemed unlikely to be a message of any great importance or surely the information would have been given by letter.

Was it a tease — a simple puzzle that the writer, Allen, had expected Laurie to be able to decipher?

Randall made another attempt to do so

for himself and for an hour tried transposing different letters for figures and vice versa but at the end of that time he was still unable to make any sense out of it. Why then should Laurie have been expected to be able to translate it? There had to be an explanation somewhere. He turned back to the opening inscription. 'Knew this book would interest you' and ending with 'Warmest regards'.

Warmest regards? Hardly the expression of a mere acquaintance — almost certainly that of a close friend or an erstwhile colleague. He was impressed by the flowing formation of the handwriting and thought back to his own struggle to write legibly at speed. This 'Allen' would certainly not have had that problem.

Would not? Perhaps it should be 'did not'? The writer sending the book to his friend — a postmaster at a small town might well have have been a telegraphist too. Could this suggest a clue to a possible solution?

He became quite excited. Having been a telegraphist himself, surely he would be on an equal footing? Struggle as he might, he could not at first see any connection between the letters and figures, for they have entirely different Morse coding. But wait! It was a regulation that at the completion of each message, any figures therein have to be repeated. To save time, these are signalled in an abbreviated form, and most of the abbreviated characters could also represent letters.

Hastily he wrote them down with their abbreviated Morse signals and their letter equivalents thus:

| Figures | 1 | 2 | 3 | 4 | 5 |
|---|---|---|---|---|---|
| Morse abbreviations | .- | ..- | . . . - | . . . - | . |
| Letter equivalents | A | U | V | none | E |

| Figures | 6 | 7 | 8 | 9 | 0 |
|---|---|---|---|---|---|
| Morse abbreviations | -... | -... | -.. | -. | - |
| Letter equivalents | none | B | D | N | T |

Now he copied the cryptogram, placing beneath each figure, the equivalent letter for each abbreviated figure signal.

S 5 5 P I G 5 N D 1 R O H 2 R S E
E P A G E N D A R T H U R

7 2 R 9 5 0 0 K 9 T W S B U R N E
T T K N T W S

'See page ND Arthur Burnett kntws'. Obviously not quite right. The 'N' and 'D' after page should obviously be figures. He checked back to the equivalents. 'D' was 8 and 'N' was 9, and in the last word 'kntws' the 'T' could correctly be replaced by a 'nought' or say — a letter 'O'.

Thus the message read: 'See page 98 Arthur Burnett knows'.

He quickly opened the book at page 98 and there at the end of a sentence he read . . . 'nobody actually knows' and these words had been faintly underlined. He turned to the beginning of the chapter which was headed, 'The Monomotapa and other Native Kings'.

He quickly scanned the first few pages wherein it was suggested that the Monomotapa (Zimbabwe Ruins area), was possibly the ancient land of Ophir, source of King Solomon's wealth, and that golden treasure might still come to light there.

The author then touched on the well-known belief that the last great Matabele ruler, Lobengula, had possessed a large quantity of uncut diamonds. Matabele men had worked on the Kimberley diamond fields and rumour had it that at the completion of their contracts, everyone of them was expected to secrete and bring back a diamond for the king. *L143,780/AFD*

It continued: 'Towards the end of the Matabele War, Lobengula, now ill, retreated northwards with his impis, hotly pursued by his enemies. It was said that at some time during this flight a single *induna* (chief) accompanied by four *maholi* (serfs) had buried the king's valuables. On their return to the camp the four menials were immediately put to death by the king's executioners. The king himself succumbed to his illness shortly afterwards and the identity and fate of the trusty *induna* remains a mystery. It has been suggested that a coloured man, named Jacobs, a confidant and adviser to the king also knew of the hiding-place, but this is conjecture and it may well be that nobody actually knows.'

Burnett apparently knows! Or at least 'Allen' believed he did!

Whoever is Burnett? and why should it so interest Laurence Maidwell and his friend? Randall pondered. Obviously a friend of theirs or at least an acquaintance. Even to Randall himself there seemed something vaguely familiar about that name, though try as he might he could not immediately recall the connection.

He put away the book and for the next hour or two attended to his business, for he needed to complete an article on which he was working, but his mind would not concentrate on it, and all afternoon his thoughts returned constantly to his earlier puzzle. There had been something in the papers about a person with that name. Yes! That was it. Now he remembered. A certain Burnett had been in the news some weeks back. It had been while he himself had been on a week's break to South Africa, and he had read about it in their Press. A man had apparently been lost in the bush and his dead body found some weeks later. The remains had been brought back to Bulawayo and the inquest held there. As far as he could recall off-hand, the coroner's findings had been 'Death by misadventure — the deceased having died of thirst.'

The name was not an uncommon one and Randall had no reason, apart from coincidence, to connect the two, yet his curiosity was aroused and he dearly wanted to satisfy it.

Why not ring Maidwell at Banshabi, where he was postmaster? But what excuse could he give for taking such a liberty? Say he was writing an article about the danger of going into the veld alone and asking if he thought it had been the same man whom he had known. He would tell him how he had deciphered the cryptogram. That was sure to interest him. It was still some twenty minutes before five o'clock and there should still be someone there in the office. How he wished he had his own phone, but knew the little that he used it would not warrant the expense. He made sure he had some silver in his pocket and made his way to the nearest call-box, booked the call and waited, well knowing the difficulty in getting a call through to these small towns. The minutes ticked by, and it was not until almost five o'clock that his call came through.

'May I speak to Mr Maidwell please?' he asked.

'I'm sorry, Laurie left the service some months ago. He accepted a very good offer with the S.A. Railways as a station foreman,' the speaker told him, and went on to explain that he didn't know his present address but that Maidwell's aunt, who lived in Bulawayo, would know, and suggested he contact her.

Well. That was that. The woman who had sold up was Maidwell's aunt apparently and goodness knows where she might have gone to. Yet he was intrigued to prove or disprove a connection between the Burnett mentioned in the book and the dead man. Perhaps Miss Maidwell was still in town. He glanced at his watch — 5.10 p.m. Would there be anyone at the auctioneer's at this late hour, and would they divulge to him, a stranger, the address of a client?

The phone was answered almost on the first ring. He imagined the clerk with hat and jacket donned, on his way to the door and cursing beneath his breath at being so delayed.

'I am sorry to trouble you at this late hour,' he apologized 'but I bought some books at your sale yesterday and inside one of them I found a note which is obviously very personal and I feel I should contact Miss Maidwell about it and wonder if you could tell me where I could find her?'

Well, it was true enough. Let him think it was important to her and not to him, and he might get the information he wanted.

There was silence for a moment, then he heard the receiver being lifted again.

'Miss Maidwell is leaving on Sunday morning's boat train for the United Kingdom. You should be able to contact her at twenty-seven Gordon Avenue, Petersdorp, where she is staying with a friend,' he was told.

The final word was clipped as the instrument was slammed down, precluding the possibility of any query or acknowledgement.

He didn't blame the clerk — indeed was surprised that he had been given the information at all.

Learning something about Maidwell, his friend Allen, and perhaps even of Burnett, was now a possibility, providing of course, that Miss Maidwell were prepared to see him.

Tomorrow, Saturday, he had no commitments and would at least try to speak to her.

# 3

When Randall woke next morning he wondered how he could broach the subject of her nephew and the others to Miss Maidwell. Would she be an old spinster virago and send him packing for his impertinence? It certainly wouldn't create a favourable impression arriving in his Velox in its present filthy condition. It was high time it had a clean and polish, so after breakfast he set to, and what a job he made of it! It hadn't looked so smart for years — and on being ashamed by hearing one of the African houseboys remark to another in the vernacular, 'that he must be going to sell it', he made a mental note to clean it more often.

He left at about ten o'clock for the address he had been given, which was barely three miles away, past the cemetery — the dead end of town — as one of his table companions always referred to it.

'Miss Maidwell?' Randall queried,

raising his hat to the middle-aged lady who answered his knock.

'I'm Mrs Hudson, but I will call her for you. Just a minute.'

A few moments later, a prim small woman, of uncertain age, and upon whose tiny nose a pair of pince-nez seemed precariously balanced, regarded him quizzically.

She estimated her caller to be in his middle twenties. He was fairly short and lean of stature. Wiry, she thought. Yes, decidedly wiry. His mouth, though a little straight, suggested tenacity of purpose rather than hardness, for any suggestion that it might indicate the latter was dispelled by his blue eyes, which deep-set under heavy brows were lively and cheerful. His bearing was courteous and his dress neat. Miss Maidwell quite took to him, and she considered herself a good judge of character.

'I am Miss Maidwell. What can I do for you?' she introduced herself.

'I am hoping that you can give me some information regarding your nephew Laurence, and his friendship with a certain 'Allen',' he told her. 'If you can spare me a few minutes of your time, I will explain my interest.'

'Come into the lounge. I was just about to have morning tea. You will have a cup with me? My friend is going to town.'

The words tumbled out one after another. She exuded excitement and fun — even her eyes and voice seemed to smile. She indicated a comfortable chair.

A slinky, short-haired and high-stepping black cat entered the room. It rubbed itself against Randall's legs in passing, as a tentative test and seemingly satisfied, returned and repeated the operation, its tail vibrating in apparent ecstasy.

'Eboneza has taken to you,' Miss Maidwell remarked pleasantly. 'He is very fussy and doesn't normally take to strangers. You must consider yourself favoured. We called him Ebony, being all black but when we discovered he was a Tom we decided on Eboneza.'

Randall bent down and stroked it strongly. The cat raised itself onto its hind legs and caressing his shin again, commenced to purr.

'I think cats intuitively know those who like them,' he suggested, taking the seat his host had proffered.

No sooner had he settled himself comfortably than Eboneza leapt delicately onto his lap, kneeded his thighs gently a few times with claws barely unsheathed, and curling itself into position, purred a little, blinked, and closed its eyes contentedly.

Without having waited for an order the houseboy had brought in tea for two. Perhaps he had intended the second cup for Mrs Hudson, but that lady after excusing herself had already left.

Miss Maidwell drew the trolley towards her. 'Milk?' she asked.

'Please.' Her guest accepted, gently adjusting Eboneza's position to one less likely to upset his tea should the cat suddenly decide to stand up.

'Now, tell me what you would like to know,' his hostess asked, handing him his cup.

Randall explained how he had come to purchase the book, what he had read in it, and what he had deciphered.

'I am curious to know whether you think that there is any likelihood of the Mr Burnett, who died so horribly in the veld recently, being the same person known to your nephew and Allen.' he asked.

She pondered this for a moment or two before replying.

'Certainly, until now, I had not connected the dead man with the one they knew. I barely knew him at all. But the Christian names are similar. Yes, I think it is a distinct possibility — a probability even,' she went on. 'My nephew Laurence and Allen Welch were learner telegraphists in the English postal service together. They both applied for posts in the Rhodesian service and had been accepted. While living in a boarding-house in Bulawayo they had met Arthur Burnett. I can't honestly say that they were particularly friendly with him. He had been here some years, having come up from South Africa and he generally gave the impression of being contemptuous of newcomers. My nephew positively disliked him, but Allen tolerated him, and because of their mutual keenness for rugby (which Laurie did not play), they became reasonably friendly. The last I heard of him was that he had gone Gatooma or Hartley way and I suppose that is why I didn't connect him with the Bulawayo inquest.

'Laurence was transferred to the Eastern Districts about the same time as Mr Burnett left, and Allen stayed on in Bulawayo until he resigned from the service, when he also went up country, though I don't know what work he was doing there. Presumably it was from there that he sent the book to Laurie.'

She continued. 'I came out to Bulawayo to keep house for my bachelor brother, but he has recently married and taken a position on the Copperbelt. The house lease was up and I decided to return to England so sold up my furniture — Oh! and my brother's damaged gun. Amongst my own books were a few that my nephew had left with me when he joined the S.A. Railways. I presumed that he no longer wanted them. I am afraid that that is all I am able to tell you, but

Laurence is coming up to see me off tomorrow and perhaps you would like to see him for yourself?'

Randall stood up, carefully lowering Eboneza who all this time had remained peacefully on his lap.

'You have been most helpful. I'm sure you could ill afford the time you have given me, leaving tomorrow as you are, and I would certainly very much appreciate your introducing me to your nephew. I look forward to seeing you again at the station tomorrow then.'

The interview had been most satisfactory. It now seemed more than probable than the dead man, Burnett, was one and the same that the two men had known.

# 4

Randall had no intention of intruding upon the privacy of last-minute farewells at the station, so he arrived there some thirty minutes before the boat train's scheduled departure.

As he had expected, at this time of the year the train bookings were light, for holidaymakers would not willingly choose the approaching English winter for their visit. Checking the passenger booking list displayed on the platform, he noted Miss Maidwell's carriage and compartment number. A 'coupé' he noticed — so only two persons in the small first-class compartment.

Bottom bunk too. The booking clerks were considerate and though one could specifically ask for a certain bunk reservation, one's age or infirmities influenced their decisions in making allocations.

He found the compartment and noticed

that the passenger had not yet arrived. Miss Maidwell's was the only name on the reservation card clipped to the window, so unless there were a last-minute booking it seemed she might have the compartment to herself.

A few minutes later she arrived, accompanied by a man about Randall's own age, who was carrying her small case for her. A station porter was attending to the stowage of her heavier luggage.

This was without doubt her nephew, Laurence. They could easily have been mistaken for mother and son — albeit rather a young mother. He had the same neat, small and precise features as the aunt. He was a little darker than she, and rather taller — perhaps 5 ft. 10 ins. or 5 ft. 11 ins. The suggestion of height being exaggerated by his slimness. A neatly trimmed and narrow moustache emphasized his obvious care for detail, but it was his voice that indicated his breeding. Well-bred, but of a family of limited means, he obviously had not received the benefit of a public school education or surely he would have chosen a more rewarding career than one in the postal service, Randall concluded.

Miss Maidwell recognized him at once and introduced him to Laurence. It seemed she had already apprised him of Randall's interest in him for he greeted him warmly and readily agreeing to have lunch with him, arranged to meet at the Railway Refreshment Room as soon at the train had departed.

Wishing her *bon voyage* and a happy retirement in her home country he excused himself and left Miss Maidwell with her friends.

★  ★  ★

He had just finished a cup of coffee when Laurence Maidwell arrived.

'Will you join me in a cup?' he invited him.

Maidwell declined. 'We had tea just before leaving for the station but it was kind of you to invite me to lunch and I shall enjoy that. However I should like to leave shortly after the meal. I had intended returning immediately after the

34

train's departure, for although I am only just over the border, it's a journey of some two hundred miles, and I am on duty again tonight at eight. My car is outside so if you like to lead the way I will follow you.'

Randall agreed. 'We can't have lunch for an hour yet though and it's hardly worthwhile going back to my flat, I suggest we go straight to the restaurant where we can chat over a drink meanwhile.'

They set off in their respective vehicles towards the town centre. The jacaranda trees lining both sides of several of the streets were past their pristine splendour, but the fallen flowers had laid a broad carpet of a beautiful misty mauve.

Being Sunday, there was little traffic and ample parking was available outside the restaurant, but the small bar adjacent to the dining-room was well patronized with regulars.

They found an unoccupied table in a corner sufficiently far from the hubbub at the bar counter. Most of the talk there centred on sport — those who were not actually out in the wonderful weather partaking in games spent much of the late Sunday morning discussing them.

They gave their order and when their beers had been served Randall brought up the subject of Burnett's death, explaining how he had become interested after decoding the message.

Having sampled their drinks, Maidwell set about explaining how the three men had become associated, and what he knew of the other two's movements since they had left Bulawayo.

'I don't know how much my aunt has told you,' he began, 'but it was rugby that brought the other two together. They were extremely keen players, and quite good too — in fact I believe that Burnett actually played provincially when in South Africa. They both played in the scrum-half position for opposing teams. Burnett was forced to give up the game though. He had broken his arm twice — the second time rather seriously, this occuring when playing against Allen's team. Allen had just tackled him when the scrum wheeled on top of them both and

Burnett's arm was fractured again. There was not the slightest hint of foul play and Burnett never suggested otherwise but I think Allen always felt a little guilty about it, as though he had been responsible, and I believe that it was this concern that accounted for their continued association — I wouldn't describe it as a 'friendship', for they were quite dissimilar in character. Burnett was dour, secretive — a loner. Allen was light-hearted, happy-go-lucky, always feeling the next field's grass might be greener. He was prepared to take a risk — a gamble, as witness his throwing up his secure career in the government service to take up a mine job at the Lucy's Luck.'

'Did they go to the mine at the same time?' Randall queried.

'No. Burnett had been there some months before he told Allen about the vacancy,' Maidwell continued. 'Coming out to join the service together, I suppose it was natural that Allen and I should remain friends, though I shouldn't describe even our friendship as 'close'. When we first arrived we were both keen to learn all we could about the country and spent some of our time 'prospecting'. We didn't know anything about the subject of course, but many of us single young men poked about optimistically, always hoping that we might just chance on some wonderfully rich gold-reef that everyone else had overlooked! During our short statutory holidays we visited most of the ancient ruins together.

'I could never condone Allen's scratching about them, even if it had not been prohibited — which it was — but I am afraid he did, and in one (I won't say which), he actually found a dozen gold beads.'

'You kept in touch though?' his host asked.

'Not regularly,' Maidwell told him. 'After I had been transferred I didn't see him again for some while. In fact the first I heard from him for months was when I received that book from him. I read the message at once of course.'

'It seems to me that the scope of such a code is extremely limited — after all, there are but eight letters covered by it,' Randall interjected.

'Yes, that is so,' Maidwell agreed, 'but it was only intended as a bit of fun. Welch thought it up when as a youth, in the boy scouts, he learned the Morse Code for his signaller's badge and later when we were learner telegraphists together we passed notes to one another in the code. We tried to use words with several of those letters. The vowels A.E.O. and U are there and most words have one or two of them. The four consonants T.N.D and B are are also surprisingly common. As you have already discovered, where we couldn't code a letter we left that letter as it was and by joining all the words together made it a little more difficult. You admitted it took yourself some hours to break it and you an ex-telegraphist!

'I think one of the reasons he put the message at the back of the book was because, by coincidence, most of it could be put into the code, and also of course for a bit of fun — to see if I remembered it.'

'You haven't seen him since then?' Randall asked as the other paused.

'I was coming to that,' Maidwell continued. 'After I had been offered my present position I spent a few days with my aunt and as Allen had something to attend to in Bulawayo, he arranged his visit to coincide. I jokingly commented on the cryptogram in the book and teased him for being gullible. He seemed to take umbrage at this, and went on to tell me that he was sharing quarters with Burnett when the latter suffered a severe attack of malaria which developed into black-water fever and became delirious. He had babbled a lot about 'hidden treasure' and called out what sounded like 'where is it? you damned kaffir' and again 'what can you do with it? I could get rid of it for you' or words to that effect. He had also mumbled some native words, which he, Allen, didn't know the meaning of, and he had concluded from all that, that it must have been Lobengula's hoard that Burnett had been referring to. He admitted that neither before, nor after his recovery had Burnett ever mentioned the subject. Allen said that he had once, very cautiously, touched on the matter and Burnett had brusquely turned the conversation away from it. I told Allen that I thought he had taken Burnett's ramblings too seriously, for in delirium one often has weird and improbable fantasies.

'He seemed annoyed at my making this assumption and our parting was a little strained, which was a pity.'

★ ★ ★

They noticed that the chatter at the bar was by now much more subdued as customers made their way to the dining-room. They rose and followed them, where an undersized but cheerful waiter, smiling broadly, showed them to a table.

'Your table taken Mister Randar,' he apologized. (His tribe being unable to pronounce the letter 'L').

'You lunch here regularly?' his guest asked.

'Only on Fridays and Sundays, but I always have my evening meal here — with the exception of Sunday night, when dinner is not served.'

They enjoyed a pleasant meal discussing various topics of mutual interest, but once they had finished their coffee it was obvious that Maidwell was itching to be on the road, though he would have been very embarrassed had he thought his host had noticed it. Sensing his guest's anxiety, Randall attracted the waiter's attention, initialled the bill presented, and suggested that they be on their respective ways.

He thanked Maidwell again for sparing him his time, accompanied him to his car and made his own way home.

# 5

Randall would have been quite unable to give any positive explanation for his continued interest in Burnett's death.

However, two points stood out clearly. Burnett was believed to know the whereabouts of a very valuable hoard and his death had been a terrible one, and bearing in mind his experience, totally unexpected. Could there have been any connection? Had he been actually in search of the first when he had met the second?

It certainly would be very interesting to learn the details and the best way to satisfy his curiosity would be to check the newspaper reports on the case.

Accordingly, on Monday morning he called at the offices of the Rhodesian *Daily News*, telling them only that he was checking on some details. He was courteously received and a youth was assigned to him to help in his search.

Together they descended to the records room. The approximate date of the paper's coverage having been supplied, it took them but a few minutes to trace the relevant issues.

Ignoring the first report of the finding of the body, he turned to the issue following the coroner's inquest. Here, as he had expected, the paper had recapitulated the full story as it was known.

'Arthur Burnett, aged 34, had been a storekeeper on the Lucy's Luck Mine. He was a spare time prospector and small-worker and had recently re-opened an old abandoned mine, the Mamba's Hole, in the district of the Lucy's Luck, but not on that company's claim area. Mamba's Hole was not yet producing and he was still in the process of clearing out the old shaft and sampling veins, but believing that the results of his assays had warranted it, he had resigned his position as storekeeper and had started to work the Mamba's Hole full time.

'There had been an unfortunate and fatal accident there a little before his own death and it is believed that a charge of

44

criminal negligence against him had been considered.

'It was not known why he decided to come to Bulawayo and set off on a short prospecting trip from there, but that is what he said he intended doing. He had come to the yard of Short and Stander, the transport contractors (where he was well known apparently), and asked if he could be given a lift on one of their trucks which was operating on the Victoria Falls route.

'All he had with him was a 9.3 mm Mannlicher rifle, a rolled blanket, knapsack, prospecting pick and his water-bottle, which held about a quart. He was obviously travelling light for a man who was prospecting and this point had been raised by the driver during the journey. To his query, Burnett had explained that he expected to be out for a few days only and had enough food for that period. If necessary he intended to trade any game he might shoot for something at a village. It had been his intention to return to the main road and await a truck lift back to town. The driver had felt concerned that the man had intended being away for a few days in such exceptionally hot weather, yet had taken only a quart of water, but presumed that Burnett knew the area and would know where he would be able to replenish his supply.

'Nothing more was heard of Burnett until his corpse was found about forty miles from the road some weeks later. It was in an appalling condition, putrefaction being well advanced, and the attention of birds or small animals had assisted in its mutilation.

'It happened that two natives had been looking for wild honey and had been following a honey-guide bird in the light forest country many miles from their village. Having found a hive in a hollow tree, one of them had gone some way to look for a dead sapling which they could prop against the tree and use as a ladder. He had made his way over to what looked to be a suitable one when he noticed the stench of a dead animal. A few yards away he discovered what it was — the remains of a man.

'A rifle was lying nearby and some

articles. Neither he nor his companion touched anything. They did not open the hive, which of course they should have done, for the honey-guide (which eats the bee larvae), will feel he has been cheated and may lead the next man to a poisonous snake or a lion. Perhaps, after all, he surmised hopefully — as they had not chopped out the nest, the bird may think that they had failed to see it and so will not be vindictive to the next people who follow it.

'The coroner had let them ramble on, knowing that by letting them tell their tale in their own manner he would be more likely to get the exact report of what they had found and what action they had taken. Indeed there was little more to come from them, for they had hurried back to their village and reported their find to the headman who had sent a cyclist to the nearest police post.

'After photographing and searching the site, Inspector Sturman and Sergeant Steyn had collected the remains and made their report. A map depicted the area where the body had been found. A postmortem was performed and though the body was putrescent the pathologist had pronounced the cause of death as dehydration. Thirst. 'Death by misadventure' had been the coroner's verdict.'

Randall closed the files.

'It's my opinion,' volunteered the youth, completely ignoring the surgeon specialist's findings, 'that he was bitten by a mamba.'

This remark elicited no comment and deep in thought, Randall left the office. Instead of his curiosity having been satisfied it had been aroused still further, for the map had shown that the area in which Burnett had been found was roughly in the direction in which Lobengula's retinue had been travelling during his final flight.

Randall considered the problem. It was all very well, his feeling dissatisfied, but what could he do about it?

The coroner and the police were satisfied. Then they didn't know what he knew. But what did he know? He *knew* nothing. Welch had jumped to conclusions over an ill man's disjointed chatter.

Yet there was the suggestion — however slight — that Burnett had been on an expedition other than prospecting.

All through lunch these thoughts crowded his mind and before the end of the meal he had come to a decision. He would try to speak to Inspector Sturman, tell him about the coded message and Welch's suspicions.

*　*　*

Shortly after two o'clock Randall entered the police station. He had decided not to telephone for an appointment, it being far easier to refuse a requested but unwanted interview made that way. He was still undecided as to how he should broach the subject. Each approach that he considered seemed less likely to arouse an interest than the last. He had brought the *Dissertation* with him of course, and hoped that he would at least be heard. Even at the last minute he almost turned back, his courage failing him, but pulling himself together he entered the office marked 'Enquiries' and addressed a

49

junior officer at the desk.

'I understand that Inspector Sturman recently investigated the finding of the body of an Arthur Burnett. I have something of interest which I think may have a bearing on the man's death and wonder if the inspector could spare me a few minutes.'

He gave his name.

The officer returned shortly. 'Inspector Sturman will see you,' he said.

The office into which he was ushered was bright and sunlit and overlooked the City Hall gardens — an oasis of shady palms and flowering shrubs. The swish of the fountain could just be heard between breaks in the traffic. The pavement on the garden side, presented a brilliant display of massed blooms — the stock-in-trade of the African flower sellers.

He had no time to dwell on such attractions.

Inspector Sturman indicated a chair and glowered at him. This seemed an ominous start. He was a large man of military bearing and past middle age. His greying hair of which there was little sign of thinning, was cut close. His eyes regarded the other steadily. Hard, efficient, but probably fair-minded was Randall's initial assessment.

His speech was precise and clipped. 'Take a seat, Mr Randall. I hope you have something important to impart. I have very little time to spare as I leave for a few days' holiday at Umtali tomorrow and still have much to get through, instructing my deputy and tidying up.'

Randall produced the book, opened it at the cryptogram and gave his interpretation of it. Sturman heard him out without interrupting.

'Then what are you suggesting, Mr Randall?' he asked.

'I thought that there might just be the possibility that Burnett's death was not entirely accidental,' he answered. 'Perhaps some Africans loyal to the old king's memory, knew what he was after and killed him somehow. After all — Lobengula himself had exacted a vicious retribution upon the village charged with the care of his own father's grave — and that merely for permitting a grass-fire to pass over the area!'

Sturman silenced him abruptly. 'Look, you are wasting my time. That message was a joke — a lark — between a couple of men acting as kids. So! Suppose this chap Welch did genuinely believe Burnett knew something. Then he was mistaken. As Metterlink said, 'nobody knows', and take it from me, in all probability there was nothing to know, for that so-called tin of diamonds is a myth. Would you take seriously the delirious ramblings of a very ill man? With regard to Burnett's death, there is absolutely no suggestion of anything other than natural causes. I won't say that he just ran out of water. He may well have had a recurrence of his malaria and been laid up for a couple of days, and was just too ill to travel, but there was no outside influence. Now forget it. I have enough work to get through during the rest of today without being worried by crack-pot amateur sleuths.'

Sturman stood up to indicate that the interview had terminated. Randall had no alternative but to do the same. It was obvious that he had made no impression on the inspector, and he resented the man's attitude.

Perfunctorily thanking Sturman he left the building.

Making his way towards his flat he reflected on the interview.

Of course the police would only act on facts — he realized that — but was it asking too much for Sturman to have shown just a little interest in his, Randall's theories? 'Mere coincidences' Sturman had inferred. Certainly there were not going to be any new enquiries instigated by the police.

Well, there was nothing to stop him making a few on his own account.

He would very much like to know, for instance, what kind of accident there had been at Burnett's mine, the Mamba's Hole, and what evidence the police had for suggesting that negligence had contributed to it. His time was his own, and he would enjoy a trip into the country. Tomorrow he would go out to the mine and try to find out something about it.

# 6

After a fairly early breakfast he left by car for what he expected to be a two-hour drive.

Before leaving the town proper, he crossed the White Stones River, now entirely dry. How different from eight months ago, when he had gone to watch it in spate, pouring over the bridge! In a few months' time it would flood again and within a few hours return to merely a stream.

Another mile, through a residential suburb, and he was on the main road and glad to to be able to put his foot down. The first few miles of the road always depressed him, passing as it did the large cement works on the right. What few scraggy bushes there were, were permanently covered in grey — the colour of sickness.

He wondered whether the trees were stunted because of the dust or whether growth was generally poor in areas where limestone, suitable for cement making, predominated. The latter he presumed, for when well past the factory he noticed no improvement.

He slowed to allow two crows, breakfasting on a mangled rodent, to fly to safety. Now *there* was a bird that knew how to enjoy life! Most small birds had to forage for food most of the day, but crows always had time to play. He had often watched them cavorting, 'weaving baskets', in thermals.

A number of them used to feed from spilled grain outside a warehouse near his flat and he recalled how one morning he had been disturbed by the frantic barking of a small dog as it chased and leaped up at one of the crows. The crow flapped slowly a few feet above the ground just out of reach of the dog and quite obviously was deliberately teasing it, for it adjusted its speed to that of the dog. Day after day, for perhaps a week, it tantalized the dog, after which time the game ceased, the dog failing to put in an appearance though the crows continued to feed in the road.

Could a dog 'lose face' and sulk?

The two crows cawed. He liked to think in appreciation of his concern for their safety, rather than 'what the Hell did you disturb us for?'

The terrain was improving now, and on his right he saw the turn-off to the Dhlo Dhlo ancient ruins, contemporary with those at Zimbabwe. He had often visited the latter but never the former, and made a mental note to do so in the near future.

Another half-hour's travel and he crossed a small river and estimated that he had covered two-thirds of the way to the mine. Some twenty miles further, the turn-off to the mine was indicated by a rough signboard, and following this unmade and dusty track for a few more miles he came upon the workings.

All looked quiet and there was little to show that it was actually a mine that he was approaching — there was no mine headgear for operating a hoist and no ore-crushing stamps. These would have to come later, when the owner had considered that the value of the gold reef warranted the expense.

Presumably Burnett would have followed the usual 'small-worker's' procedure — should the vein indicate likely commercial values, he would take samples of the quartz to his bank for assay and if satisfied, they would then grant him a loan for the purchase of the machinery.

As it was, there was merely a windlass over an open shaft, a couple of corrugated iron sheds, and a sun-dried brick 'office' and several native huts built of the same material.

He noticed a native woman scouring some pots outside the 'office' so went over to that building, the door of which was open. An elderly African heard his foot-steps and came to the door. An office it might have been, but now it was a residence, for the caretaker had taken it over as such in preference to his hut in the compound. He was now the 'boss' and as long as the man in the bank paid his small wage, that was where he would live.

Apparently until such time as Burnett's estate had been wound up, the bank, to whom he was probably indebted, had asked the caretaker to remain.

He wondered whether the custodian would be cooperative, but he had no need to be anxious for the man seemed only too pleased to talk, perhaps taking Randall for a possible purchaser of the enterprise. If he were not to disillusion the man he would have to frame his questioning carefully.

'I have heard that this mine is dangerous and that a man died here a little while before Mr Burnett left,' he commented.

'Yes, that is so,' the African told him. 'But it was an accident. A native by the name of Gideon, who was Mr Burnett's 'boss-boy' fell to the bottom of the well shaft and had been killed. A shackle clamp joining two lengths of steel cable had become loose, allowing a short length of cable and the bucket in which the man was being lowered to become parted from the main cable, and so crash to the bottom.'

'I would like to examine the cable,' Randall told the caretaker.

They went over to the well-head and

the man unwound a few yards from the windlass.

'You will see,' he explained, 'that the bucket has been reconnected to the cable, for Mr Burnett had to go down the well to retrieve the dead man's body. At first he made a loop in the cable for his foot but once at the bottom he rebolted the length of cable still attached to the bucket, to the rest of the cable so that he could bring up the body — but I will show you how it parted.'

About twenty feet of cable attached to the bucket had been joined to the main cable with steel shackles. One of the bolts in the windlass section had loosened allowing the bucket section to fall. The two lengths of cable had been joined by doubling back a few inches of one end into a 'U' and clamping it with a bolted shackle. The other end of the cable had been threaded through the 'U' and also bent back and clamped with a shackle.

Randall examined the ends carefully. The cable end attached to the drum and which had become loose, was well oxidized, but the end of the piece to which the bucket had been attached appeared, on close inspection, to have been recently cut. True, the frayed ends were not bright, but they seemed to have been artificially dulled. A dab of soldering fluid (spirit of salts), would soon oxidize steel, and this appeared to have been done.

Providing there was no other reason to arouse suspicion, this could very well have gone unnoticed and the accident put down to a shackle bolt working loose and allowing the cable to part. No one would have troubled to examine the cable ends — especially the bucket end, for it had been the opposite end of the join that had slipped.

It would have been easy enough for someone to slacken the bolt a little so that with the weight of a man it would come apart.

But why shorten the cable?

While Randall's attention was concentrated on the examination of the couplings, another man had joined the caretaker.

The latter introduced him. 'This man

was the chief windlass man when the accident happened. He is still living at the compound, hoping that if someone re-opens the mine, he will be re-employed.'

Randall pointed out to him that one of the cables seemed to have been shortened recently and asked if he had any comment to make.

The man explained that in the hullabaloo of the accident he had not noticed it or even considered the possibility, but he had been greatly surprised and shocked that Gideon had been killed outright by such a fall, for the length of the cable below the join would have been about sixty-six feet so that even if the joint had slipped as soon as the unwinding cable cleared the drum, he should have fallen approximately twelve feet, for the well was only about seventy-eight feet deep to the bottom, where the horizontal tunnel was being driven.

But the length of the cable below the join was now only about twenty feet, so that when the join cleared the drum and parted, he would in fact have fallen some fifty-eight feet. He could not say when any alteration had taken place.

Out of curiosity, Randall unwound the rest of the cable on the drum, and noticed one other join. This was quite secure.

No wonder the police had been considering a charge of criminal negligence! Surely it would be against mining safety regulations to join a cable in this manner if it were intended to support a bucket in which a man was lowered.

It was too much of a coincidence, both a loose shackle bolt which would have caused a nasty accident, and a cable shortened by forty-six feet which would have ensured the accident being a fatal one. There was little doubt — this had been murder!

Randall asked if he could look around the property. If he could find the missing length of cable he would have something to go on. He spent some time examining the workshop, which was full of the usual mining impedimenta, old wheels, broken jumper drills, hammers without handles, lengths of old piping of assorted sizes and various lengths of wire and wire rope cables. These latter he examined carefully, laying out on the sand beside the shed any pieces of the same type as that on the windlass. There were no lengths of anywhere near forty-six feet, and such as there were had obviously not been cut for years.

Having failed to find any trace of the missing length of cable in the workshop, he turned his attention to the immediate area adjacent to the mine, poking about under bushes and in the long grass. He came across several narrow cuttings, two or three feet wide and several yards long, and varying in depth from three to ten feet. These had been exploratory cuttings following quartz outcrops, but investigations of all these proved fruitless. He made his way back to the mine where the two natives were still in conversation.

He addressed the windlass man. 'Do you know if there are any abandoned mine-shafts in this vicinity?'

'Yes,' he was told. 'There is a small one into which we throw our ashes and general rubbish and there are two other small ones quite close.'

'Take me to them please,' Randall asked him. The caretaker tagged along and the three of them took to the footpath which led from the compound and reached the first of the three, only fifty yards away. This was the one into which they deposited their rubbish. The edge was clear of bushes and the hole could not have been a deep one for rubbish had filled it to within a few feet of the lip. He found nothing of interest there — indeed it was hardly likely that anything incriminating would have been dropped into a regularly used tip.

They moved on to the next. This was barely one hundred yards from the first but there had been no regular passage of feet to wear a path to this one. The edge was screened by weeds, scrub and grass, so that only a small hole in the centre was visible. Examining the edge carefully it was evident that the tips of some of the bushes had been broken, and not recently, for they had shrivelled, a state indicating that it had occurred some time ago.

Randall explained what he hoped to find down the hole and set about clearing some of the scrub where the edge seemed fairly firm, but found after doing so, that the lip was too crumbly to be approached safely. The bottom was still mostly obscured and appeared to be about twenty-five to thirty feet.

How many of these exploratory shafts have been dug following a promising quartz vein only to peter out fruitless!

The windlass man left them for a moment and returned dragging the bole of a dead tree. This he pushed out over the hole for perhaps two feet.

'If both of you will put your weight onto holding down this end I will crawl out a little and look into the hole,' he suggested.

This they did and waited tensely for his observations as he peered downwards.

'I can see a coil of something at the bottom there, but it is dangerous to try to climb down. Wait, I will fetch something from the workshop.'

He was away some ten to fifteen minutes and returned with a length of wire to the end of which he had fixed a makeshift grappling hook — a piece of thin mild steel he had bent to the shape of a ship's anchor. Crawling out again he commenced to fish, and, by good fortune, hooked a coil almost immediately and gently drew the length of wire cable to the surface.

Together they laid it out on the ground and found that it measured fifty shoe lengths — as close to forty-six linear feet as made no difference.

One end appeared to have been recently cut. If any proof of deliberate murder were required, then this was it.

The cable was coiled carefully and the two Africans were asked to see that it was put in the workshop, protected from the weather, and told that if the police asked about it, they must show it to them.

There was nothing more to be done at the mine and Randall considered his next move. According to regulations he should report his discovery to the nearest police station — the same one that originally investigated the accident, but he had something else in mind. Inspector Sturman was on holiday as from today and his junior, Sergeant Steyn, would probably be in charge. He would try to see Steyn — explain to him how he could prove that Gideon's death had been murder, then endeavour to interest him in his theory that Burnett had been doing more than prospecting when he met his death.

He checked the time. It was now past midday. If he left right away he would be home by 2.30 p.m. He gave his helpers one pound each for their assistance and went on his way.

As he drove to the mine that morning he had noticed an ideal spot for a picnic lunch — the bank of a tree-lined stream. On reaching it, he drew off the road and pleasant though it was, he allowed himself but thirty minutes for his meal and wasted no further time in reaching town.

# 7

Before going to his flat he called on the newsagent, two doors away, and asked if he might use the telephone, for the proprietor had let him use it on other occasions.

It had just turned 3 p.m. and he wondered if Steyn could fit in an interview at such short notice — or indeed, would see him at all, if Sturman had mentioned his name to him.

He was put through to Steyn almost immediately.

'My name is Randall,' he explained. 'I called in and discussed the strange death of Arthur Burnett with your Inspector Sturman yesterday. I know he did not seem at all impressed with what I had to say, but I have just been out to the mine Burnett owned, the Mamba's Hole, and I found out something very interesting — something I feel sure the local police knew nothing about. It may have no bearing on Burnett's death but it most certainly does have on the death of the boss-boy Gideon.'

'No, I would rather not tell you on the telephone,' he answered in reply to Steyn's question. 'Could you please spare me a few minutes of your time to discuss it with you?'

Steyn's voice, though indicating little enthusiasm, certainly lacked Sturman's abruptness and he agreed to an interview, fixing the time at four o'clock. That suited Randall well. He was able to take a bath, change and still have ample time.

Arriving at the station a few minutes early he was recognized by the junior officer who had shown him into Inspector Sturman's presence on the previous day and the slight wry smile with which he was greeted suggested that he had either overheard Sturman's sermon or that the inspector had made some comment to him concerning the interview. There seemed no intended insolence about the smile — rather a little sympathy. No doubt he too, had been subjected to his superior's cutting tongue at some time!

Steyn must have advised him that Randall was expected, for he was at once ushered into Steyn's, or rather Sturman's office, for the former had taken over that room in his senior's absence.

Steyn rose, introduced himself and indicated a comfortable chair.

Rather thick-set and apparently stolid, Styen's swarthy skin and dark pencil-thin moustache contrasted surprisingly with his rather fair hair. Any suggestion that his heavy features, thick lips and slowness of speech might indicate a lack of sharp intellect was quickly dispelled by the keenness in his eyes and precision with which he expressed himself.

He addressed Randall with a pronounced South African accent.

'Now say what you have to say briefly and quickly. As you know, I have two persons' work to cope with. My superior did comment briefly on what you told him about your interpreting those coded lines in the old book. He didn't give it much credence I can assure you. The autopsy and inquest left no doubt as to the cause of death. However, it is a coincidence that the area in which the body was found was roughly — and I emphasize, very roughly, in the general direction in which the old king could have been travelling.

'Then too, there was his boss-boy's accidental death. Am I right in thinking that it is some information concerning that death that you have unearthed?'

'Yes,' Randall acknowledged. 'I am certain that the man's death was no accident, but had been deliberately contrived. I have spoken to some of the workers and they also feel that my interpretation of the 'accident' is the correct one.'

He went on to give a detailed report of what he had discovered at the mine that morning, remembering to mention that the forty-six feet of cable had been retrieved from the sampling shaft and had been safely stored under cover.

Steyn was silent for a few minutes. 'If what you say you have discovered is confirmed, then a case of murder is certainly indicated. Of course this branch did not handle that investigation, and I will pass on the information to the officers concerned. The forensic department will certainly be able to match up the cut ends of the steel rope and will be able to determine whether the cuts were recent.

'Incidentally, why didn't you report your findings to the Repton police?'

Randall had of course anticipated the question.

'Firstly, Repton was out of my way, and besides, I still feel that the murder may have a bearing on Burnett's death, which your department handled. Perhaps some friend or relative of Gideon, believing him to have been murdered, had managed to trace Burnett and taken his revenge.'

Steyn shrugged. 'I have seen the report you made to Sturman and can only repeat what he told you — there is not the slightest suspicion of foul play. Coincidence — yes. Direct connections — no. I'll just get the file.'

Returning in a few minutes, he placed a large bulky envelope beside him and proceeded to open a folder. He mumbled to himself for a few moments as he read through the report of the finding of the body and the inquest. Deciding there were now some facts perhaps unknown to Randall, he began to read aloud.

'Burnett had died practically insolvent. His earnings from employment on the Lucy's Luck had been poured into his own venture. Monies that may be received from the sale of his mine machinery and his rifle — which was an expensive make — will be used first to pay any outstanding wages due to his workers and any bank overdraft, and the few other small creditors will have to share the balance *pro rata*.'

He reached over for the envelope.

'These few personal items we intend to send to his next of kin.' He continued. 'The only relative that we know of is a brother somewhere in Australia. He too, it seems, is a bit of a rolling stone and we are trying to trace him through the Australian police.'

He prised open the adhesive tape sealing the envelope flap and shook from it four articles. A gold signet ring, a small silver medallion about the size of a half-crown, engraved 'To Arthur — Good Luck', a stag-horn handled pocket-knife with about a dozen implements and a silver pocket-watch — a Waltham Hunter. A small tag attached to this latter bore the inscription 'Found in the grass fifteen feet from the body'.

Randall casually handled the watch. It was a type very popular at the beginning of the century which he recognized as similar to one his father had owned. The back would have a double case. He remembered how his father had often opened it to show him the inscription his employer had had engraved on the inside of the case when it was presented to him, marking thirty years of service.

Automatically his thumb nail felt for the catch that would spring it open. Inside, and carefully cut to fit the shape of the outer casing, was the photograph of a young lady. Mother when young? A girl friend?

He hooked his nail beneath its edge and lifting it from the watch, turned it over, curious to know if the identity of the person was revealed.

No endearing message there. Not even a name — merely two short lines of letters and figures.

He was at once impressed by the similarity that these bore to those inscribed in the old book he had bought at the sale.

K171059G1
598W102G5

Mentally he transposed the known letters for the figures, as when abbreviating them in Morse, as he had done before. He noticed that none of the four letters in these groups KG and WG had any figure equivalents, so concluded that they would have to be left as they were, as indeed he had had to do with several letters in the first cryptogram.

Thus he interpreted it as:

KABATENGA
ENDWATUGE

He looked about him for something to write on. A small desk calendar was at his right. He fingered the top two spent leaves.

'May I?' he asked.

Steyn nodded and pushed his pen across.

Randall tore the two sheets from their mounting and copied one of the lines on each, putting his translation beneath and excitedly passed them over to Steyn.

'See what this is? It is another example of the cipher used by Welch in the Metterlink book. This watch obviously belonged to Welch so he must have been to the spot where Burnett died.'

'Mr Randall,' Steyn interjected brusquely, 'You have a vivid imagination haven't you? Inspector Sturman felt the same about you, though I doubt if he anticipated that we would be seeing you again. You surmise that it was Welch's watch because of the words on the reverse of the photograph. Even if that were so, there could be many explanations as to how Burnett came to have the watch in his possession.

'They were friends — or at least close acquaintances and Burnett may have been given it by Welch, or bought it from him, or for that matter even stolen it from him — he certainly was hard up.'

He went on: 'What did you say you did? Write articles for papers and magazines? Well this one you can leave alone. You certainly seem to have unearthed a case which might well prove to be murder at the Mamba's Hole, and we are not ungrateful for your having given us this information, but there is nothing to suggest that Burnett's death was anything but accidental or that the verdict reached at the inquest was the incorrect one. With Burnett dead, and seeming to be the obvious suspect, if Gideon has indeed been murdered, there is no immediate hurry to raise the issue. Sturman will be back on Monday. It can wait until then. It's a problem for the Repton police and he can pass it on to them. In the meantime, forget about being a sleuth will you. Go write a story about the Queen of Sheba.'

Was Steyn genuinely annoyed by his interfering? Randall certainly felt the last few remarks to have been unnecessarily sarcastic, yet the police sergeant had seemed to take an interest in all that he had told him, and that included his deciphering of the inscription in the watch. He was expected to keep his own nose out of the business, but had a sneaking feeling that Steyn might not be averse to making a few enquiries of his own.

This assumption appeared to have been borne out, for on collecting together the contents from the envelope, Steyn reached across and retrieved the two slips of paper on which Randall had done his decoding and was just about to put them with the other items when Randall interrupted him.

'Just as a matter of curiosity, Mr Steyn (he was still unsure as to the title by which he should correctly address him) have you any idea what those two words mean?'

For a moment he thought he was about to receive a curt response.

'Excuse me a moment,' Steyn asked him, and left the room.

He was away several minutes and

returned with a middle-aged African clerk.

'Most of our young constables appear to have been recruited from this area and other places along the line of rail. This man comes from the western district.'

He handed the two slips of paper to the man and asked him, 'Do these two words mean anything to you?'

The newcomer examined the first. KABATENGA. No sign of recognition crossed his features. He looked at the second. ENDWATUGE. Surely there had been a sudden stiffening of the body? An almost imperceptible sly glance at the two men? Only for a second, and directed primarily at Randall, as though Steyn he trusted, but not this stranger.

But it was fleeting, and Randall knew that he may well have been mistaken, for it was the reaction he had been hoping to see.

'They don't seem to mean anything, sir. They are just two African names,' and he politely put the slips on the table and stepped back to await permission to leave.

That Steyn had given no indication

that he had noticed anything about the man's reaction did not necessary mean that he had not done so. He was more used to native mannerisms than was Randall, and no doubt, to hiding his emotions.

'That's that then, Mr Randall.' Steyn rose and extended his hand. 'Thank you for coming to see me. It has been interesting. Good afternoon.'

As Randall passed through the 'Enquiries' office he borrowed a pencil from the duty clerk and hurriedly wrote the two words on the reverse of an old envelope. He must not forget them.

# 8

It was now Wednesday morning and nearly a week had passed since he had purchased the *Dissertation* . . .

Steyn had suggested, or more correctly instructed him, to leave the matter well alone. What was there for him to do anyway? There was certainly one thing he did want to do. He wanted to find out how Burnett had come to have Welch's watch. The obvious way was to go out to the Lucy's Luck mine where Welch was working and ask him. No. He couldn't do that. Just presume for a moment that he, Welch, were involved in something illegal. It would be wrong to alert him to the fact that the watch had been found. No, he would have to avoid any mention of the watch.

He could still go out there to see him. Pretend that he was up that way on some business — tell him of his purchase of the book and explain how, being an ex-telegraphist, he had managed to decipher the coded message. He could tell him that he had actually met his old friend Laurence Maidwell. He needn't say he had arranged the meeting. Let him think he had met him accidentally at the sale of his aunt's property. That would give him the opening and he would play his cards from there.

He prepared a flask of coffee and some sandwiches for his lunch, for it would be extremely unlikely that he would be able to get a meal of any sort at the mine, and the nearest small town, Repton, was many miles beyond the mine turn-off.

He reached the branch road to the Mamba's Hole, where he had interviewed the caretaker on the previous day, without incident. Three miles further on he came to the Lucy's Luck turning. Four miles more and the mine buildings came into sight. He was surprised at the size of the mine, expecting it to be much smaller.

Before reaching the mine proper, he came to a building bearing the sign, 'Mine Boarding House'. Many of the larger mines had such establishments. Though described as 'boarding houses' it was seldom that they actually accommodated any of the staff overnight, but most of the unmarried men who lived in the single quarters had their meals there.

Leaving his car in the shade provided by a massive wild fig tree, which considerately had been left adjacent to the verge when the road had been constructed, he pushed his way through the swing gauze doors of the veranda and addressed himself to whom he rightly presumed to be the superintendent.

'Can you kindly tell me where I can find Mr Allen Welch?' he asked.

'Welch? I am afraid you won't find him here at all. He left — let me see — I should say about six or maybe seven weeks ago. Went prospecting on his own I believe.'

Randall must have registered his disappointment.

'Tell you who could probably help you though,' his informant added as an afterthought, 'Ralph Westlake. He is on afternoon shift. Starts work at three o'clock so should be about. He was in for breakfast anyway. His room used to be next to Welch's and they often came in to meals together. I should try him.'

Thanking him, Randall strolled down to where the single quarters had been pointed out to him by the superintendent. Seeing a native servant sitting on the veranda edge and lethargically polishing a pair of shoes, he asked him to indicate where he could find Mr Westlake. Following the youth's direction he approached the open door of one of the rooms and interrupted a man who was reading the previous day's newspaper.

'Mr Westlake? My name is Randall.' He held out his hand. 'Hope I am not intruding but I was expecting to find Allen Welch here at the mine but have been told that he has left and that you might know where he could be found.'

Westlake's handshake was firm and friendly. 'No intrusion at all.' He smiled. 'Take a chair. I'm glad of someone to chat to. The day-shift are working, and night-shift are sleeping. As regards Welch's present whereabouts, I am afraid

I can't help you though. A friend of yours was he?'

This was embarrassing. Randall was anxious not to reveal the real reason for his interest in Welch, yet loath to be deceitful to this amiable man.

'Well no — I know little about him actually. Knowing an old friend of his I thought I would look him up,' he said uneasily. 'He has actually left then?'

Westlake nodded in agreement. 'He resigned some time ago. Gone off into the bush somewhere. He used to spend a lot of his spare time scratching around — so-called prospecting. Always hoping for the big strike of course. Most of them did it. Even those whose interest lay mainly in shooting could seldom resist picking up the odd piece of quartz if they found one. The usual glitter turned out to be 'fool's gold' — iron pyrites, but there was always the chance that one day it might be the real thing.

'This time though, Allen had seemed more confident. He had sold up his few personal pieces of furniture (these quarters are furnished very simply by the company you know), and had left here in his usual 'bush' outfit. Khaki shorts, *veldschoens* and chequered weave shirt — he was rather flamboyant and always seemed to fancy that type of shirt in preference to the usual khaki shirt or safari jacket. Probably thought it added a Klondyke touch! He seldom wore a hat other than a peaked army fatigue cap.'

Randall changed his position. Though only mid-morning the heat from the corrugated iron roof and the warm air streaming in from the sun-drenched veranda made it uncomfortably hot.

'So you don't know where he went or whether he has found anything?' he asked.

'No,' Westlake told him. 'I can't say for sure which area he intended to prospect. Somewhere the other side of Gatooma I understood, but one of the Africans heard from another that he had moved off in a more westerly direction.'

'On foot?' Randall asked.

'No. He had an old Hillman. It was a bit knocked about but apparently reliable.'

Randall mentioned the name of Burnett. 'You knew him I suppose?'

'Oh yes. Poor old Burnett. What a horrible way to die. He used to work here, but of course you know that or you wouldn't have mentioned his name. He used to share quarters with Welch. They had known each other before — in Bulawayo, I understood. Used to be very interested in rugby. Was on the selection committee I believe but I don't think he ever played here. He had been damned ill last year, seven or eight months back I suppose. Nearly died of blackwater fever. It was touch and go for some days. They treated him in our little mine hospital. We don't have a resident doctor — he visits only once a week and serious cases would go to the general hospital in town. In his case our nursing sister thought it risky to move him. You know, with blackwater there's not much you can do — you either get over it or you don't, and our nurse has had considerable experience. I would put my trust in her any day.'

This then must have been the illness that Welch had mentioned to his friend

Maidwell. The one when Burnett had been delirious and had rambled on so, and had talked about the things that Welch had hinted at in the cryptogram at the back of the book.

Would it be presumptuous of him to speak to the nurse about it, he wondered. He decided to do so.

He could think of no good reason to offer as an excuse for his wanting to see her, so making no mention to Westlake of his intention, he bade him farewell, and leaving his car still where he had parked it, set off on foot.

A little beyond the boarding-house were three or four detached bungalows in spacious grounds — the residences of the managerial staff. The gardens carefully tended, the lawns immaculate, and obviously benefiting from the copious supply of water pumped from the mine daily, which otherwise would have run to waste.

He had no trouble in locating the hospital — a fairly old building, and almost certainly built originally as the mine offices. It was supported on brick pillars and surounded now, by a fly-screened veranda.

Blue gum trees shaded the building on two sides and except for the base of these, where the grass was starved of nutrient, the lawns here too, were green and lush.

Two large sprinklers, one on either side of the drive were, even now, drenching the thirsty ground, the limits of the spray lightly touching and refreshing him as he approached the entrance. Though far from modern, the building was in a state of good repair and an atmosphere of cool restfulness pervaded it.

He mounted the steps and pushing past the glazed swing-doors, turned again momentarily to look over the mine complex, still undecided as to how to frame his questions without inviting a rebuff.

The nurse must have watched him coming, for he was startled when she suddenly addressed him from behind. 'Can I help you?' Then as he turned, continued, 'We don't normally allow the visiting of patients until the afternoon, but if you have come from a distance I will stretch a point.'

She smiled. 'Whom do you wish to see?'

She was in her forties but still very attractive. Her nurses' cap failed hopelessly to contain the mass of her thick, dark brown hair. She was perhaps a little plump for her small stature but it seemed to suit her. Her cheerful manner and kindly voice immediately dispelled much of his anxiety.

'I haven't come to see a patient,' he explained. 'I came to the mine to meet Mr Welch who was a friend of the late Mr Burnett but find that Mr Welch is no longer here. I am writing a magazine article on the dangers of people going out alone on prospecting and hunting expeditions — Mr Burnett's case is typical — and I am wondering if you might be able to give me some help. My name is Randall.'

'I'm Sister Woodcock. I don't see how I can help you, but do come in and sit down and let me know what you have in mind. I'm not busy — only two patients at the moment and neither confined to bed.'

Randall explained that he had heard of several cases of such people dying from thirst or accidents or attacks by wild animals. One man had slipped on a rocky kopje and his foot had become wedged in a crevice in the rocks and he had been unable to extricate himself. Another had been pounced upon by a lion after leaving his rifle with his kit while he went behind some bushes to relieve himself. He explained that he was particularly interested in the psychology of these 'loners', and wondered what she could tell him of Burnett's attitude, especially as in his case, he understood he had been delirious at one stage. That might be particularly revealing he thought. Normally he would not expect her to divulge any information concerning a patient, but after all, in this case the former patient was dead and his was precisely the type of case that he was researching.

She had listened quietly without commenting.

'I remember Mr Burnett, of course. We are seldom busy at the hospital except in the case of an accident, which fortunately is very rare. There is very little that I can tell you, I am sure,' she told him. 'It was months ago, you know. He was in a bad way when he was brought in — babbling incoherently.

'He had not wanted to be taken into hospital when he first became ill, but his room-mate became anxious when after some hours he was rambling, and so he contacted us. Mr Burnett was in this state for the rest of the night and well into the following morning. I was very worried about him but didn't feel that another move to the hospital in town was advisable at that time. He proved to be tough as nails though, and the following morning his temperature had dropped somewhat and he became lucid.'

'What was his manner after that?' Randall asked, for he remembered that Maidwell had told him that Welch had said that Burnett seemed concerned about what he might have said during his illness. Randall was eager to know how soon after the delirium this concern had manifested itself.

The nurse thought for a few moments.

'You must remember that I did not know him at all before he came into the ward, so I can make no comparison with what his attitude may have been before his illness and what it was then. He did seem short-tempered though, and asked me what he had been talking about while he raved. I was unable to help him there, as I had been relieved by a night nurse shortly after his admittance — she would have sent for me of course, had his condition deteriorated.

'He took no breakfast, only copious drinks, and it was after one of these that something suddenly occurred to him that he considered important. He asked if I would go over to the single quarters and bring a book for him that was in a suitcase under his bed there. I told him that I couldn't leave the hospital and would send a message and perhaps his room-mate would bring it over for him later.

'This seemed to cause him intense annoyance and as I didn't want his temperature up again, I told him that when the part-time nurse came in later in the morning I would get it for him, which I did. Yet when I brought it, he ignored it, leaving it unread on his bed-side table, between his and the adjacent bed, and was beside himself with anger, when, on awakening from a sleep (which I had induced), he found the second patient reading the book. Later on, on the same day, he reached into his trouser pocket to get some change to pay for cigarettes he had wanted, and fumbling, dropped some coins to the floor. To my surprise, one of these was, I remember, a golden sovereign. I hadn't seen one since I was a child. His ward-mate, who was not confined to his bed, retrieved it for him and passed some comment.

'At this, to our astonishment, Burnett had raged at him for interfering.'

'Tell me, Sister, did he read the book during the rest of his stay?'

'No. I don't think he did. I suppose that is why the incident stands out in my memory. He seemed so keen for me to get the book and then didn't read it, although he was in hospital for another week. It seems that he was only concerned that the book was not left in his room in his absence.'

'I suppose you are unable to tell me what the book was?'

'No. I remember that it was a very slim volume. I should say about a third to a quarter of the pages of an average novel. It had no dust-jacket, but had a hardback binding. Pale brown — perhaps sandy, would be a more accurate description of the colour. There was an emblem, such as a military badge on the front, beneath the title, but what that title was I have no idea. I do recall though, that when I put it on the table, I flicked the cover open, and noticed that the frontispiece was a photograph of a young man in military uniform, and mounted on horseback. I am surprised that I have been able to remember as much as that.'

Randall thanked her for all she had told him and assured her that he had found it most interesting and helpful.

Returning to his car parked beneath the wild fig tree, he now realized why no one else had availed themselves of the only shade in the road. Green woodpigeons, or maybe starlings, had plastered his car with their droppings. So much for Saturday's thorough wash and polish!

He drove a few miles from the mine and pulling off the road, brought the car to a stop on the shady side of a large baobab tree and took out his lunch.

Eating it slowly, he reflected on what he had learned during the morning and considered what to do next.

After perhaps half an hour's rest, he reached a decision and proceeded on his way towards town.

# 9

When Randall had passed the Mamba's Hole turn-off earlier, on his way to the Lucy's Luck, he had noticed scrawled in white paint on an old ploughshare, a sign indicating by means of an arrow, that a 'store' was situated one mile down that road. Indeed he remembered seeing it when he had visited Mamba's Hole on Wednesday and had already decided that it might be of interest to meet the storekeeper, so took that turning when he reached the sign.

He pulled up outside the store. It was a typical 'kaffir truck' establishment. There was very little stock of any one thing, but a wide range of individual items to do with daily living, and the inevitable coloured small tin trunks so loved by the Africans for taking back to their villages after perhaps a couple of years working on a mine, and containing all the purchases they had made over that period.

A stocky, ginger-haired man came out from the building as the car pulled up and extended his hand as Randall left the vehicle.

'McGregor.' He introduced himself, warmly squeezing his visitor's hand in a grip surprisingly powerful for an otherwise slightly built man.

Without waiting for Randall to declare the reason for his call, the storekeeper hastened to explain that not many Europeans shopped at the store — for that matter not many Africans did either, except after the mine pay-day at the end of each month, when he was rushed off his feet, for there were several small-worker mines in the district.

Now being a slack time he welcomed any caller.

Inviting his guest into the single living-room behind the store, he asked him to take the more comfortable looking chair. What the customer had come in for could wait until later. The opportunity for social contact was the more important.

'Have a small dram with me?' he invited his new acquaintance. 'I've only whisky — can't keep beer cold. Having no fridge I can't stock anything that won't stand some heat. By the way, I don't normally start drinking at this time of the afternoon. One each evening is my quota, but I get so few visitors with whom I can enjoy a chat over a drink.'

Many old timers, 'bush-whackers', did take to heavy drinking in their isolation but McGregor did not appear to be in this category and Randall believed him, for there was no sign of the slovenliness either in his person or his establishment which would have been expected in such a case.

He had noticed on his arrival, a couple of half-caste children, who had quickly scurried behind the building, and they too, had been neatly dressed and clean.

If McGregor had chosen a simple African woman for a companion, that was his own affair. Randall had spotted a small but well-built shack to the rear of the shop, and no doubt both he and his spouse were happy enough, but one could understand his longing to converse in his own tongue whenever possible. Unlike most Scotsmen, he had almost lost his accent, and but for his name and the use of the word 'dram' he might well not have been recognized as a Scot. He had probably left Scotland as a child, or even more likely, been born in Rhodesia or South Africa.

Out of courtesy, Randall joined the storekeeper in taking a whisky and explained that he was keen to hear anything of Burnett, who had owned the Mamba's Hole mine. He did not tell him of what he had found to interest him in the book bought at the sale, nor reveal his conviction that Gideon had been murdered.

He did feel some shame in pumping him for information without being open himself, but in telling McGregor that he hoped to write an article about Burnett's death, he was telling the truth, for he had made up his mind that he would, eventually, do just that.

'It seems a coincidence to me,' he went on, 'that within a few days of Gideon's death, Burnett meets his own, especially when, as I understand, the police had suggested that there might be a case of criminal negligence brought against him.'

'Strange that you should be asking about Gideon,' McGregor suggested. 'Of course he had shopped here as nearly all the Africans around here did, but some days after his death his widow had come to the store to see me. She was obviously nervous about something but eventually produced a Queen Victoria golden sovereign, in mint condition, and asked if she could spend it.

They all trust me around here, and knowing that I give them a square deal, I get some natives from as far as the Lucy's Luck coming to shop here, rather than at their own store, and that's about ten miles away.

'Naturally I was surprised and somewhat suspicious about the sovereign. Being in that condition I feared it might have been stolen from a collection so I asked her where she obtained it. She explained that her late husband had had it in his possession. He had visited his home village during the previous year — perhaps eight or nine months ago, she could not remember exactly. Gideon's brother had given him two such coins and asked him to find out if they could be spent in shops, but he, her husband, had been frightened to try to spend them in case he had been accused of having come by them dishonestly.

'But now that her husband was dead she was short of money and had risked coming to him knowing he would advise her.

'Well, it was only one coin, and after all, I had no reason to believe that it had been stolen, so I helped her out. She made some purchases and I gave her the change. I suppose you are wondering if I gave her the full present value of the coin? As a matter of fact, I did give her a fair price. Perhaps not quite what she might have received from a collector but more than she would have got from a hard-headed dealer.'

McGregor rose, and unlocking a small safe produced the gold coin for Randall's inspection.

The hearing about two such coins in the one day was surely more than coincidence, Randall conjectured, but he made no comment.

He very much wished that he himself could have asked the widow some questions, and would particularly like to know where the late Gideon's brother was living.

'I suppose the widow is no longer at the Mamba's Hole compound?' he asked his host.

'No. But she is not far away,' he was told. 'I don't know where she comes from, but there is a woman from her own village married to someone at the Lucy's Luck, and until Burnett's estate is wound up she intends to stay there with her. Naturally, she is hoping that eventually she will get some compensation for her husband's accidental death. I expect you would be able to find her if you went along there. I must make it clear that I wouldn't have told you all this if I didn't trust you not to make trouble for her.'

'You can rest assured on that point,' Randall hastened to put his mind at rest. 'I shall give her every help I can — getting her into any sort of trouble is the last thing I want.'

If he purchased something for her at the store he would be serving two purposes, for he could hardly leave McGregor's without buying anything, and he had already made up his mind to return to the mine and try to trace her.

'I would like to visit her and take her a little gift. What would you suggest?'

'It depends on what you consider 'little'. When she came in to spend that sovereign she looked longingly at a certain dress I have here. She held it up to herself half a dozen times but knew she couldn't afford it and had to settle for the necessities she had come in for. It's priced at four pounds.'

Randall stood up. 'I'll take it,' he said, extracting his wallet, 'and I'm very grateful for the help you have given me. Thank you also for the drink.'

He was happy that he had been able to kill two birds with one stone and just hoped that he would be able to find the woman, otherwise disposing of the dress would be a little awkward.

McGregor accompanied him to his car, obviously loath to see his departure.

'Call in and see me again any time you pass this way won't you?' he called after him.

As Randall reversed, he heard a giggle and two small heads poked around the side of the store. The happy, carefree smiles of two delightful little coloured girls cheered him on his way.

★　★　★

Reaching the main road he glanced at his watch. 3.30 p.m. already and about ten miles further to go. Unconsciously he increased his speed a little and fifteen minutes later was within sight of the fig tree under which he had parked in the morning. He certainly wasn't going to make that mistake again, and drove on to what he could see was the mine compound on the far side of the mine itself.

He pulled up outside a building

bearing the inscription 'Compound Manager', and finding the door open, knocked on the frame.

Receiving an invitation to enter he introduced himself.

'My name's Randall. I am a part-time writer and have been researching into the death of the native, Gideon, at the Mamba's Hole, as I understand the police have suggested that criminal negligence was a possible factor, and I am wondering if there is a story for me there. You know McGregor's store near that mine I presume?'

The compound manager nodded in assent but made no comment.

'Well,' continued Randall, 'McGregor told me that Gideon's widow is living here with a friend or relative and I would very much like to talk to her.'

'Hrmph,' the other grunted. Slim and tall, his upright bearing and general manner bore the stamp of an ex-police officer. Now in his middle fifties, he had probably taken an early pension from that service.

'And what do you hope to learn from

her — supposing that she is actually living here?' he asked abruptly.

Perturbed somewhat by the man's officious attitude, Randall explained. 'I would like to assure myself that her husband's death was not in any way contributed to by his own negligence. If it were, it might affect her claim for compensation — if not, I may be in a position to support her case.'

The impression he was creating did not appear to him to be a very favourable one, so he was agreeably surprised with the compound manager's reply.

'You realize that we do not allow Europeans in the African compound? There's a room at the rear of the office here where you can speak to the woman if she can be found.' He looked at his watch. 'This office closes for general business at five sharp.'

He turned and called in a uniformed African assistant and instructed him to find and bring in the widow.

Some ten minutes later he returned and ushered her in.

She was slim for an African woman of

her age and of lighter skin than the local tribes. As soon as she spoke it was obvious that she had had a certain amount of education and spoke English fairly well. Randall himself was reasonably fluent in Sindebele but this was obviously not her language.

Realizing now, that she was more sophisticated than he had expected, he began to wonder what attitude she would adopt when later he came to present the dress to her.

Having assured her that he was in no way connected with the police, or indeed with any authority, and would give her all the help he could in fighting for a fair compensation for her husband's death, she talked freely in answer to his questioning.

'Gideon had been boss-boy at the Mamba's Hole mine. Mr Burnett had valued him as he had worked for many small-workers and knew much about the gold reefs in this area.

'One day he had rediscovered the gold vein, the loss of which had been the cause of the previous owner abandoning the mine. His employer had rewarded him with five pounds and they had drunk together. At first it was only kaffir beer and as he Gideon, was not a heavy drinker he had soon become light-headed and given Mr Burnett one of the sovereigns, and on being asked where he had obtained them, he had merely said that he had been given two by someone. His master had become very excited and had pressed spirits on him, and plied him with questions, and he feared that he may have divulged too much. He might even have mentioned his brother's name and other things that his brother had spoken secretly to him about, but could not recall all that he had said before he passed out.

'All this he told me on the day after he had traced the lost vein, for on that day he was very worried on his brother's behalf. He was also unwell from having had all that liquor and he had not gone to work.'

'And I suppose it was shortly after that when the accident happened?' Randall prompted her.

'No. This had been several months

before Gideon had been killed, and while Mr Burnett was still working on the mine here — the Lucy's Luck. He was at that time only working the Mamba in his spare time.

'Ever since that night there had been tension between them. On numerous occasions Mr Burnett had pumped Gideon for information as to where the coins had come from.'

Anxiously Randall's eyes sought the office clock. What he was being told was most interesting but he did not comment.

The widow continued: 'About a week after Gideon's death, his brother, Kabatenga had also died suddenly at their village. This surprised me, for only a short while before, a friend had come from that area and had said how well he had looked.'

Randall could hardly hide his excitement! Kabatenga! That was one of the two words he had deciphered from inside the case of the watch that had been found close to Burnett's body.

He interrupted her: 'How is it that he was Kabatenga, yet your husband, his true brother, was Gideon?'

'Gideon was his first name which he took when he came to get work. His tribal name was Kabatenga. He was Gideon Kabatenga. He was known as Gideon.'

'Tell me,' he asked her, 'as your husband's death occurred some months after he had given his master the sovereign, do you think that it could in any way have been connected — presuming of course that his death was not an accident?'

She looked sadly at her questioner. 'I feel strongly that his death was no accident, but what advantage could it have been to anyone? No. I cannot think that the sovereign had any connection.'

Randall encouraged her to continue. 'Did anything unusual happen immediately prior to the accident that could have had any bearing on it?'

'No. I cannot think that their relationship was in any way noticeably different — but yes, there was one small thing perhaps. Gideon had asked for a week's leave to go home, and on the following day his master had asked to see his *chitupa* (Identity certificate). As you will know, this must be produced when a worker is signed on for employment or signed off when it ceases, at which time it is again dated and signed by the employer, but Mr Burnett had never asked to see it since my husband had begun work there about a year before. This had occurred about two days before his death. That was the only unusual thing that happened.'

Randall considered. This might well have a bearing on the 'accident'.

'What was his tribal district?' he asked her.

'Bamatuzi Tribal Trust area,' she told him, and explained roughly where it was, adding as an afterthought that they came from Changa's village.

She continued petulantly: 'What do you hope to learn by all these questions? Always people are asking questions. First it was the police officer with an African policeman on the day my husband died. Later came another white man who I think must have been a police detective. He was not in uniform but detectives do

112

not wear uniforms do they? Now yourself.

'I did not intentionally mention the gold coins to any of them as I was frightened, but I have told you about them because you said that Mr McGregor had already done so, and you have been kind.'

Noisy and exaggerated movements in the office next door were no doubt to draw his attention to the time, which he now perceived was only a few minutes to five o'clock.

He thanked the woman for giving him all the information, and with some apprehension, he now handed over the packet containing the dress, explaining that it was a little present in appreciation of that assistance. In the event, he need not have been so anxious, for although her immediate attitude had suggested a certain reluctance to accept it, on peering into the bag she recognized the dress as being the one she had wanted so much at McGregor's store, and realizing that McGregor had in some way been involved, was obviously overjoyed to accept it.

Acknowledging her thanks and assuring her of his continued help he showed her to the door.

The compound manager, now satisfied that he was not going to be delayed after all, turned from the window and his feigned contemplation of the mine's extraction plant and extended his hand cordially to Randall.

Through the open door, Randall perceived that a set of golf clubs was already being loaded into a car outside. He smiled, and warmly thanking the eager golfer for his co-operation, got into his car and made his way homeward.

# 10

Randall had much to think over during the journey. It was obvious that until he had checked the *chitupa* Burnett had not associated the name Kabatenga with Gideon, yet he obviously knew that the coin was in some way connected with that word, having mentioned it in his delirium, for otherwise Welch would not have known of it.

From the same source, the *chitupa*, he would also have learned of the district that the two brothers came from. Why then had he gone to where he did — some two day's walk from the area which one would have expected him to make for?

He very much regretted that the nurse at the hospital had not been able to give him the title of the book.

From her description of it, it certainly was not the *Dissertation* that he had bought at the auction. Not that there was anything in that book which could have helped anyone searching for hidden valuables. Even the slight reference that the book had made to Lobengula's hoard had referred to uncut diamonds only. There had been no mention of sovereigns, so there was little likelihood of any connection there.

Even as he mused, the short twilight had faded and night had closed in.

A ghostly spectre materialized before his windscreen. He jammed down his brake pedal, slowing just sufficiently to avoid killing a pennant-winged nightjar that now floated up and to one side, lifting and falling with each wing-beat like thistledown in a gentle breeze, the single delicate, eighteen-inch feather at the extreme tip of each wing streaming gracefully with each movement. Truly a beautiful bird.

Another thirty minutes and the lights of the town could be seen. He passed the extension of Acacia Avenue in the 'Suburbs' down which was situated the house where only a few days ago he had attended the auction. How he would have liked to have seen that book that the nurse had mentioned!

Perhaps the library would have a copy. It was not very likely though. From her description it appeared to have been a privately and cheaply printed short autobiography — not the kind of volume they would stock. Bookshops? A possibility, but it had not seemed like a recent publication. Somebody must have a copy. What about that chap in the bank, Rutherford? He collected *Africana* (old books specifically associated with the continent of Africa).

If the house sale last Thursday had not been on a work-day, Rutherford would have assuredly been there himself. Though not close friends, Randall and he were certainly acquainted.

He did not immediately garage his car, but left it in front of the flats as he would be needing it later to go for his evening meal. After showering, changing, and ensuring that he had some coins in his pocket for the telephone, he made his way to a nearby call-box. Looking up the number he wanted he dialled. It was so long ringing that he was on the point of hanging up when it was answered.

'Rutherford here. Sorry I was so long.'

Randall made himself known. 'You may vaguely remember me. I have spoken to you occasionally when we met at sales, though I think we have never been introduced.'

'Yes. I remember you well. Peter isn't it? I read your articles. Jolly good too. I enjoyed that amusing one about the baboons some weeks ago particularly. What can I do for you?'

Randall told him of his interest in the slim book he had heard about and described it, but omitted giving any detailed explanation of his reason for such interest.

'Yes, I think I know the book, and have a copy,' Rutherford acknowledged. 'If it is what I am thinking of, it is a short biography of a young man who came out about eighteen-seventy — dabbled in general trading among other things. Joined the police for a while and was caught up in the Matabele War of eighteen seventy-three. He was a member of the party that had pursued Lobengula and died the following year from natural causes. He had kept up a detailed correspondence with his family in England and one of his brothers collected the letters, collated the material, and had it published privately as a memorial to him. It has some quite detailed maps pin-pointing his various excursions.'

'I wonder if I could call in and have a look at it?' Randall asked him.

A few moments silence followed. 'Tell you what,' Rutherford suggested, 'I have to go out as soon as I have dressed — have a dinner date. As a matter of fact I was in the bath when you rang and that is why I kept you waiting so long. If you could come around straight away, I will let you borrow the book.'

A glance at his watch showed Randall that he could well spare half an hour and still be in time for dinner at the restaurant.

'Very kind of you. I'll come right over. I have your address from the directory,' he told him.

Within fifteen minutes he was at Rutherford's, where he was met on the threshold and the book handed over to him.

'You can let me have it back any time. It is of little value and there are a number of them about, but this one is in particularly good condition.'

They walked out together to their vehicles, chatting about the various purchases each had made at sales and how profitable or otherwise some of them had proved to be.

To his dining companions at the restaurant, Randall imparted little of what had transpired during the day. One showed more than a passing interest in the book and expressed a wish to borrow it, but on learning that it was only on loan he did not press the matter.

Before returning to his flat Randall called at a convenient garage and topped up with petrol and oil, having already decided what he would do the next day, and knew that it might mean a long drive before he came to a garage again. He would go out to the Bamatuzi area and ask a few questions concerning Kabatenga's death — an accident, Gideon's wife had suggested. He had no idea what he expected to find or what he intended to do there.

What was that other name on the slip of paper enclosed in the watch? Endwatuge? Who or what was it? No one seemed to know, or if they did, had not mentioned it. Pity he had not mentioned it to the widow. She might have known. It must have had some significance for the older native in Steyn's office — of that he felt sure.

It was about 8.30 p.m. when he arrived home and he spent the next hour collecting together anything he might need on a trip which could last two or three days.

The only ordnance map of the country that he owned was one on a small scale, giving very little detail but it clearly showed the Bamatuzi Trust area, and a single track road leading to that district. He would have to follow that road and make enquiries as he went along.

At 9.30 p.m. he turned in with the

book he had borrowed from Rutherford.

The contents were much as had been described to him by the lender and he could well understand why it had had a limited circulation. The maps, however, were well detailed showing exactly where the skirmishes in which the trooper had been involved, had taken place. He had not been on the Wilson patrol (which had been close on Lobengula's heels and had been completely annihilated), but he had visited the spot in the following year and both his, and Wilson's routes had been meticulously recorded and mapped. The positions of small streams, hills, wagon tracks and villages had been faithfully pinpointed.

Checking against his ordnance map, Randall confirmed that both these routes passed close to the area he intended to explore.

There certainly had been no indication given as to where anything of value might have been hidden.

Where was one thing. *What* was quite another!

One chapter had seemed significant

and he turned to it once more. Bearing in mind, that as far as he was aware, only sovereigns were involved, what he read left him reasonably certain that he now knew their original source.

No wonder Burnett had been concerned about leaving the book in the room he shared with Welch!

His suitcase had probably been locked — yes, but almost any case key fitted another. Reading the chapter might well have given encouragment to someone who, though suspicious, might not otherwise have taken his feverish ramblings seriously.

It had been a long and tiring day. He switched off the light and within minutes unconsciousness enveloped him.

He was being lowered down a deep well by bucket and windlass. There was nobody operating the handles which spun freely. He dropped hundreds of feet to the well bottom and found himself in hospital. He recognized the nurse from the Lucy's Luck hospital. All around the walls of the ward were one-armed bandits — slot machines. These took only sovereigns and each time he pressed the buttons, instead of coins, fruit tumbled out. Apples, pears, plums.

Why no mangoes, guavas, pineapples? He went from one to the other pressing the buttons but now only springs and pieces of wire flew out. Lengths of wire cable were all over the room, enmeshing him in the coils.

He struggled to free himself and awoke in a sweat — his sheets twisted and tangled around him.

He went to the bathroom, took two aspirins, straightened his bedding and at last fell into a deep and untroubled sleep.

# 11

It had been his intention to rise early on the following morning but the sun was already streaming through his east-facing window when he woke. A glance at his watch showed it to be half-past six and he had expected to have left town by then but the long rest and sound sleep had been beneficial, indeed needed, and he felt considerably refreshed. He washed and shaved quickly and took down his .410 bird gun which he hurriedly cleaned and oiled, having overlooked that chore when making his preparations the night before.

Not being in the habit of taking a cooked breakfast, his meal took but fifteen minutes. He did not trouble to fill his Thermos this time as he intended making tea or coffee as and when required on this trip, and had stowed a two-gallon can of fresh water in his car before retiring.

He checked that his two-pint water-bottle was also filled, locked up and had left the flat within an hour of waking.

The day promised to be a scorcher and he was thankful that the sun would be behind him as he travelled and so he wouldn't have to suffer the discomfort of it shining straight into his eyes whilst it was still fairly low.

Traffic was already building up as he reached the outskirts of the town for most shops and businesses opened at 8 a.m., but as his route did not pass through the industrial district he was at least spared the hordes of bicycles he would otherwise have had to contend with.

For the first thirty miles he had the benefit of a good tarred road which served the farms, but after that, the road degenerated into a sandy track. At this point he pulled up to consult his map and satisfy himself that he was still on his intended route.

It was certainly warming up and even at that hour could be heard the isolated stridulating of cicadas — another hour and their noise would be piercing.

Two native cyclists skidded to a stop in the soft sand, drew up alongside him and alighting, enquired as to whether he were in trouble. He thanked them for their concern and in turn, asked them if he would reach Changa's village by the road he was following.

'Carry on for a little while and the road will fork. Take the left-hand track and after about one and a half hours' travelling you will come directly to the village,' they told him.

'Do you mean one and a half hours on foot, by cycle or by car?' he asked in all seriousness.

'By bicycle,' they explained.

Randall thanked them again, and remounting their heavily overloaded cycles they went on their way.

One and a half hour's cycling on that sandy track would mean about fifteen miles he calculated, plus the few before the turn-off — say twenty miles. In the event he had travelled almost thirty before reaching the outskirts of the village.

Understanding the African's reasoning,

he quite expected it to be much further than they had said. They reasoned that you hoped that the distance you had to travel would be short — you hoped to be told it would be short, therefore it would be ill-mannered to disappoint you and tell you that it would be long.

This he had allowed for.

A few excited youths and children gathered around his car, any unexpected happening demanding their full attention. He wondered why they were not at school and was surprised to find that it was already past ten o'clock and this was probably their mid-morning break.

He asked them where he might find the headman, Changa, and his house being pointed out to him, he parked his car and made towards it. He had gone only a short distance when an elderly but striking figure came towards him, having no doubt heard the approach of the car.

The few wispy hairs on his unshaven chin were flecked with white. He was over sixty, Randall estimated — an African of a bygone generation, both in age and character. He was taller than most of his tribe, and although in European attire (but his feet unshod), he nevertheless presented a certain savage dignity of bearing.

'We see you!' Randall greeted him in the vernacular.

'We see you,' Changa replied, and first one and then the other responded with the formalized and correct greetings and replies that etiquette required as a prelude to the discussion of routine business.

'I am not from the police but have come from the mine at which one of your villagers worked and was killed. You will have heard about it no doubt. His name was Gideon Kabatenga. I think it is probable that his death was not an accident as had been claimed,' said Randall broaching the subject.

Changa made no reply, as indeed none was as yet called for. Randall had merely stated a fact.

He continued, 'I believe that his brother also died recently in this district. Sometime before he died he told Gideon that he had found something of great value and I am wondering if he had been killed by someone because of what he knew.'

Changa tensed and looked uneasily about him. 'It is hot out here in the sun, let us go beneath that tree,' and he indicated a huge mango tree close to his house. A low mud wall extending from the wall of the house formed a rectangle which enclosed an area of perhaps a quarter of an acre. The tree was within this enclosure which ensured a measure of privacy, and under the tree, a large log, polished by considerable use, served as a bench.

Once they were seated, Changa continued. 'The police came here and examined Kabatenga's body and say that he too was accidentally killed.' He shuffled his bare feet in the sand and was obviously acutely embarrassed.

'It was no accident. He was killed, but not by any man, but by the spirit — the oracle of the hill. You are a white man and cannot understand these things that happen. Perhaps they only happen because we believe these things, but I will tell you what I know. Every bone in his body was broken. It was as though an elephant had taken him up in its trunk and smashed him to the ground.

'No human could have done that, and there are no longer any elephants in this district. This too you should know and then may believe what I have told you of his death.

'Before the white men came there was a greatly renowned oracle which spoke from the hill Ndwatuka.' He had lowered his voice almost to a whisper as he spoke that word. 'The voice came out of the hill itself, but it spoke only in times of great trouble — a prolonged drought, a serious disease amongst the cattle or when our people should go to war. Sometimes it did not speak for years and it has not done so at all since the white men came.

'There has always been the family of Kabatenga who were great *ngangas*[1], the eldest son taking over from his father, but the rest of the family would live normally

---

[1] *ngangas*. Witchdoctors, medicine men, soothsayers etc.

in the village and have no further family association with him. The last practising *nganga* was in my own father's time. His son, Kabatenga's father, died when quite a young man soon after his own son's birth. Neither of these two was an *nganga* but in the old days the *nganga* lived alone with his wife near the great cave on the other side of the hill from which the oracle spoke, and in that cave he did what *ngangas* did. No one will go to that cave for it is on a sacred hill.'

Randall could hardly contain his excitement. That word Ndwatuka! The word on the slip of paper in the watch had been deciphered as Endwatuge, but Welch who presumably had written the coded word might well have misheard it during Burnett's rambling.

'Would Kabatenga have dared to go to the cave?' he asked Changa.

'Yes. He was not a trained *nganga* but because of his family's background, he or his first son, would have been able to go there without fear. He had not married so the line is now ended. Perhaps the spirit thought it best to end the dynasty.'

'Is the hill nearby?' Randall asked him.

Changa altered his position a little and pointing over his shoulder, he said, 'That is the hill. The one whose top is bare of trees.'

Changa would not willingly, or more precisely, intentionally, look at the hill. Certainly no native would deliberately point to it, holding it in such awe as they did.

Randall was facing it and had no such inhibitions.

'Would you kindly take me to where the body was found?' he asked of the old man.

'I have much to do today,' he was told, and calling to a youth nearby, the headman gave him some instructions.

'This boy, with others, found the body. He will show you the place.'

Randall rose and joined the youth. Too old for the local school but not yet working. The boy's fixed grin suggested a simple mind and provided the answer. Simple — yes, but obviously happy and free from the anxieties that the more intelligent are beset with. Not for him any superstitious fear of the hill. Probably nobody had ever troubled to tell him about it.

He enquired of the youth as to whether he could go part of the way by car and the answer being in the affirmative, the boy set off on foot, leading the way, while Randall followed slowly in the car along what was obviously a sledge track.

Villagers often make such sledges by cutting down a tree with a large fork. Nailing a few slats across for a platform and hitching it to an ox or a donkey, they are able to transport quite heavy loads, even in quite heavily wooded country. It was frowned upon by authority — indeed strongly discouraged, for it was a common cause of the beginning of soil erosion.

About a mile from the village they reached a partly cleared but well-shaded spot, and the tall hill, Ndwatuka, now seemed barely twice that distance away.

At this point the sledge track turned slightly away from the direction of the hill, and although apparently still negotiable by car without too much difficulty,

Randall decided to set up camp at this pleasant place and to continue from there on foot.

Having had no refreshment since leaving home, he was looking forward to this stop for tea. He indicated his intention to his companion and in no time his guide had collected dry grass and sticks, and asking for matches, soon had a blaze going. In less than ten minutes the water had boiled and tea was brewing. He poured a mugful for himself and handed the billy with the rest to the boy.

Knowing that he would probably not eat again until evening he opened a tin of 'bully', thick wedges of which he put between bread slices, making two massive sandwiches. The youth expressed his appreciation of the unusual meal by chewing noisily with open mouth and further emphasized his enjoyment by repeated and loud smacking of his lips.

Not much more than an hour had elapsed between his arrival at the village and the finish of their snack. After carefully stowing the food in his car, as a precaution against invasion by ants,

Randall asked to be taken to the spot where the dead man had been found.

Narrow sandy paths formed by cattle as they made their way to grazing, had deviated from the sledge track in several places, and they moved off down one of these, the direction of which suggested a shorter route.

The youth set off at a fast pace, his bare feet scudging up the fine sand, though whether he did this for sheer pleasure or because of some infirmity, Randall was unsure, but he dropped back a pace to prevent some of the sand so disturbed from finding its way into his own shoes.

They had not gone above a quarter of a mile when, without a word, the youth stepped off the path and approached a clearing of some three or four square yards immediately adjacent to an old maize field.

A small type of dove was fluttering desperately on the ground seemingly unable to leave the spot, though there was no apparent reason why it should not have done so. A small bird of another species was lying dead about a foot away. The boy bent down, and easing a tiny noose from around the dove's neck, killed it, and after putting the dove and the small bird into a pocket of his shorts, turned towards the path again without having uttered a word.

Anxious though he was to get to the scene of Kabatenga's death, Randall was interested in what he had witnessed, and in a kindly manner halted the boy — asking him about the snares and how they were made and set.

He explained that three or four hairs from a cow's tail were knotted at one end and then twisted together by rolling with the palm of the hand on one's thigh. One then made a running noose of about one and a half inches in diameter. The other end was bound to a short stick and driven right into the ground so that only the noose was showing and these nooses were so adjusted that they stood upright — the springiness in the twisted hairs making this possible.

Ten or twenty were placed within a few feet and a little crushed maize or maize meal was spread around. As the bird foraged and pecked at the food it would put its head through the noose and then as it walked or hopped the noose would tighten.

It was difficult to find suitable hairs, for very few cows had tail hairs long enough and some of these snares were made from hairs he had pulled from the tail of the visiting police trooper's horse, when minding it, some months previously. He rarely caught doves — usually only the smaller birds. These birds would be roasted and eaten with porridge.

The two returned to the path and before long reached the base of the hill, which was quite unlike any other hill in the area. Most of them sloped fairly gently and evenly, and were strewn with massive granite boulders, many of which were piled high upon one another. This particular hill though, rose almost sheer on this its eastern face and at the base of this side the body had been found.

There was no clue as to what had happened — not that he would have expected to find any after several weeks.

After all, he had been told that there had been no wounds — only broken bones.

He wanted to think things out on his own and was particularly eager to visit the cave on the other side of the hill.

Thanking his helper, he presented him with a few loose coins and bade him return to the village, and the boy made off in high spirits.

# 12

Now alone, Randall sat upon a boulder and with his binoculars scanned the rock face above. No ordinary person would have been able to scale it. Skilled mountaineers could no doubt have done so, and he himself might have scrambled, albeit with some difficulty, to a height of perhaps fifty feet, but from that height upwards it was sheer for perhaps a further one hundred feet.

There could be little doubt that the man had fallen from the top, which had accounted for his terrible injuries. Changa's account of his having broken every bone in his body was of course an exaggeration, but a fall from that height would certainly result in multiple fractures, more than likely neck, back and some limbs.

But why had he fallen? This was his home. He would know the district well, and according to the headman, he alone of local natives might have climbed the hill. Suicide then? Who could say? Was he pushed? And if so by whom? And what was he doing at the top of the hill anyway?

Randall adjusted his binoculars to observe more clearly five or six *dassies*[1] which were basking in the hot sunshine on a very narrow ledge on the otherwise sheer rock face, about two-thirds up the hillside.

What an easy life they lead, he thought!

They must spend some time feeding, but on the only occasions when he saw them they were basking in the sunshine. He focused more sharply on one particular animal. It was so pale as to be almost white — an albino. He had never seen or even heard of an albino rock-rabbit, but almost every species of

---

[1] *Dassies*, also known as rock-rabbits are small furry animals the size of a rabbit, but thick-set like a guinea pig. They feed on herbage and inhabit most rocky hills and are able to scale almost sheer rock faces.

animal produced this aberration from time to time. A shadow passed over the ground and in a flash, a black-breasted eagle dived at the *dassies* who, after a warning squeal from one of their number, disappeared as if by magic. He marvelled at the ability of the eagle to veer from its unsucessful dive, at the moment when impact on the rocks seemed inevitable. The *dassie* is a common food of this eagle but this time the attack was unrewarded.

Where had the *dassies* gone? He scanned the ledge carefully. A thin slit in the rock face, seemingly but a few inches in height must have provided for their escape.

He continued watching the ledge for some time, curious to see whether the eagle would return to the attack when the animals came out into the sun again.

It was uncomfortably hot — at least 100°F where he was sitting in the sun, and sweat streamed from his forehead and temples.

Mopani bees, tiny stingless insects, much smaller than houseflies, were causing him considerable annoyance by settling in the corners of his eyes as they sought the moisture there, compelling him to wave his hand continuously as he endeavoured to disperse them.

The heat and the bees became much too irritating to allow him to concern himself any further with the *dassies*, so putting away his binoculars he took up his gun and leaving the path, moved off towards the other side of the hill.

The soil here was obviously of low fertility and seemed to support only a short thick type of grass — and this in abundance. The three-inch seed carriers of the grass are barbed all their length, so that as one pulls them from one's socks a barb and seed is left — the barb point soon working through the material to reach the skin.

In no time Randall's socks were completely matted and caused such discomfort that he had to remove them, and stuffed them in his pockets. He replaced his sandshoes, for that is what he was wearing, having decided that they would be the most suitable footwear for climbing rocky hills in the course of his search.

Now having rounded the hill he discovered that the west side faced another, but much smaller hill, and was separated from it by a narrow valley of perhaps one hundred yards in width. In this stone-free, and seemingly fertile area the remains of stone walls could still be recognized, suggesting that there had once been an enclosure for goats or other animals, and the outlines of old huts were also still discernible.

Randall looked for a suitably shady spot and putting down his gun, rucksack and field glasses rested his back against a convenient rock and considered all he had been told by Changa. So this was the mysterious Ndwatuka, and on this side, somewhere, was supposed to be a cave that nobody except Kabatenga was likely to visit — and he was dead.

He decided to rest for a while and later search it out. It should not be difficult to find — and what would await him there? It had all turned out so much easier than he had dared to hope.

He drowsed pleasantly in the warm shade. Cicadas shrilled an even steady note, occasionally interspersed by the liquid notes of a golden oriole. He dozed for perhaps an hour, then leaving his other items where they were, he took up his binoculars and made his way towards the smaller hill, reasoning that he would have more chance of pin-pointing a cave from some distance away. In this he was successful, for he had climbed only a little way when, on looking across to the other hill he could plainly see the opening of a large cave about half-way up it. The roof of the cave projected somewhat over its mouth and rose sheer above it for several feet.

The sun had by now reached this side of the hill and on a narrow ledge just above the cave, another group of the ubiquitous *dassies* was enjoying its warmth.

Taking note of a particular rock as a landmark he crossed the valley again and keeping his landmark in sight, had no difficulty in climbing to the cave, having found a well-defined but long-disused path. Centuries before any Africans had used the cave, primitive man — the Bushman, would no doubt have been in occupation.

He found the cave larger than he had expected, not so deep perhaps, but wider and loftier. At the rear, a bench-like slab of rock protruded into the room but this was obviously as nature had formed it, being an extension of the wall itself. If there had ever been any wooden implements or utensils they had long disappeared. The bases and remains of a couple of large clay grain receptacles were evident and a few potsherds. All appeared to be of considerable age. The rock walls were smooth and met the floor over its entire circumference. The sun was letting ample light into the cave and he was able to examine the walls minutely for cracks, nooks or crannies — anywhere which could be a possible hiding-place. The floor was of soil built up or blown in over thousands of years and could well be several feet deep but seemed hard and undisturbed underneath the immediate dusty surface. On hands and knees he examined every inch of it from wall to wall, again and again. He sharpened a stick and tested everywhere for any place where the soil might have been disturbed recently but found no trace of that having occurred. He noticed that his own shoes, though only light, had made marks in the dust topping so even a barefooted native would have left some impression.

He closely examined the low shrubbery growing near to the mouth of the cave and clearly perceived where his feet had broken a few sprigs of the plants. There were no recently broken twigs other than those he himself had damaged. As these small plants would have grown to their present height during the last wet season it seemed logical to assume that no other entry to the cave had been made recently. This was most disappointing. His hopes had soared ever since Changa had mentioned the hill's name and particularly when he had been told of the cave.

Dispirited, he made his way slowly down the hill. His search had been thorough. How thorough he realized when checking on his watch he saw that two hours had elapsed since he had entered the cave, and the sun was well over to the west as he retrieved his gun and bag before setting off for his intended camp.

Reaching the place he set about making himself comfortable for the night. First he cleared a larger area about the spot where he had made the fire earlier in the day, concerned that when built up for the night it would not spread to where he slept. He then gathered up some dry grass which he packed down as a make-shift mattress and collected sufficient logs to last the night.

With these chores completed he made up a small fire and set a filled billy to boil. He had been looking forward to this, his first camp on his own, ever since deciding to make the trip. His only other experience of camping-out had been well organized — too well organized for his liking; camp-beds, folding chairs and the inevitable crates of beer.

As soon as the billy boiled he threw in some coffee. After a few moments he set it aside and spreading the fire a little to reduce the flames, placed the frying pan with steak, sausages and bacon on the glowing embers.

He tried to work up some enthusiasm — make out he was enjoying himself — but to tell the truth he felt somewhat disheartened. He had been so excited when he realized to what the word Ndwatuka referred and been told about the cave — thrilled when he found and actually entered it, then so disappointed at finding nothing significant there — not even a clue. No wonder he felt deflated.

It was now quite dark and he attended to the cooking mechanically. Soon an appetizing aroma issued from the pan and the fragrance of the coffee brought home to him how thirsty he really was — hungry too. He had had only that single sandwich since leaving home that morning.

He set to with gusto. If hunger were the best sauce he had ample. By the time he had finished his meal and a second cup of coffee he felt less depressed. There was no real reason to feel dispirited. Admittedly he had failed to find anything exciting, but what of that? It had, on the whole, been a most enjoyable and interesting day.

He built up the fire with the logs, for though the recorded temperature would still have been quite high, a drop of perhaps 40°F since midday was making the evening air feel decidedly chilly. He had not reckoned with that possibility and had brought no clothing other than what he was wearing — shirt and shorts. Sparks were soon shooting skywards from the blazing logs.

At the village, only a mile away, the evening meal was also under way and African voices drifted clearly in the night air — a quiet mumble, only very occasionally overlaid by a feminine giggle or a child's ejaculation. Gradually the chatter diminished and someone began to thumb a monotonous and repetitive tune of but a few notes on a home-made musical instrument. Words were fitted to the tune which continued endlessly. Yet far from being a cause of irritation the music induced a pleasant state of tranquility.

Randall spread his blankets on the grass, bunched up his rucksack for a pillow and placing his clasped hands behind his head, gazed up into the starlit sky and was content.

He thought back over the day's happenings — that magnificent black eagle soaring so majestically and scaring the life out of the *dassies*. Perhaps they didn't have such an easy time as he had supposed. They were prey to serval cats, pythons, and jackals in addition to eagles, and had to be continuously on the alert.

Fancy seeing an albino *dassie*! It was possible that he was the only European ever to have come across one. Now he came to think of it, that same animal was with the group sunning themselves that afternoon, on the ledge above the cave. Something had disturbed them then — perhaps seeing him — and they had disappeared to the back of the rock, just as they had done in the morning on this side of the hill. No wonder they had not come out from their refuge after the eagle had left — they must have some means of passing right through the hill!

The granite formation often resulted in caves, fissures etc., and these animals could penetrate surprisingly small cracks and holes, and even if they had such an escape passage, it could well be minute by human standards. Had this particular geological feature occurred anywhere other than on this 'taboo' hill, Ndwatuka, and so close to the *nganga's* cave, he would have ignored it. As it was he became quite excited again. He was not bound by time and decided that it might be interesting to have another look at that side before returning home.

Nightjars were 'churring' and crickets chirping. He remembered watching as a shooting-star, materializing from no particular spot, and traversing an arc across the heavens, disappeared as suddenly as an extinguished spark. That was the last thing he did remember before being awakened just after dawn by the barking of baboons as they sought the first sun-kissed boulders to thaw the night chill from their stiffened bodies.

He shivered involuntarily and wrapping a blanket around him made up the fire.

By the time he had breakfasted there was already a noticeable warmth in the sun. It was going to be another scorcher.

He carefully smothered the fire, packed a few items of food in his rucksack, refilled the water-bottle and with his gun and field glasses set off for the other side of the hill.

# 13

Entering the valley he made his way along the middle until he reached a position just below the cave that he had explored on the previous day.

He now turned right and began to climb the small hill on the opposite side. This hill was not as high as that in which the cave was situated and he had almost reached the peak before finding himself level with the top of the cave.

From this position he could see the ledge on which the *dassies* had been sunning themselves, though it was now in shade — for it had been afternoon when he had watched them there before. It appeared to be very narrow — only a few inches in depth, with a mass of sheer rock backing it. By climbing a little higher and examining it carefully through his binoculars he could now see that what had at first appeared to be but a few inches would prove to be much deeper for it sloped downwards — back towards the rock face.

The mystery of where the animals had disappeared to was also apparently solved for he could see a very narrow gap between the rock face and the ledge itself and though this looked too small for even these small animals to pass through, yet disappeared they had, and without leaving the ledge either to the right or to the left.

When viewed from the ground the impression had been gained that climbing to the ledge might well prove to be impossible, but he could now see that this was not necessarily so, for if one could scale the first few feet at the left side of the cave, a climber might well be able to reach it, for there appeared to be some rough footholds higher up.

Satisfied that there was at least the possibility of his being able to get there, he descended the small hill and crossed to the other, where he began the climb to the cave. On reaching it, he examined the rock face to the left. Here it bulged slightly outwards, and partly obscured by this protrusion, and leaning against the rock was the bole of a dead tree — just a gnarled stump, about four feet in length.

It had obviously not grown there but had been placed in that position to assist in climbing above the cave, yet even should one mount the log, getting up the next few feet did not appear to be a feasible proposition.

Discarding his rucksack and the binoculars, he loosened the sling of his gun, swung it across his back and started to climb. From the top of the log he was surprised to find that at about arm's length, a thin stone wedge had been driven into a crack affording an excellent and solid grip. By this means, and with the assistance of some very conveniently placed toe-holds (which surely had been improved by human hands?), he was able to pull himself up onto the cave brow. As this sloped forward great care had to be exercised to avoid slipping over the edge.

When he stood upright on this he found that the shelf upon which he had seen the animals basking was at about shoulder height.

Sloping downwards and backwards as it did, it was indeed much wider than one would have thought when seeing it from the other hill, and so had hidden from view that part of the slit in the rock face where it actually met the base, for at this point the gap widened considerably.

A large flat stone stood at one side of the opening and though this was not large enough to cover the hole completely, would, if placed across it, so reduce the opening as to make it less conspicuous though the *dassies* would still have found room to enter it. This they had most likely been doing for years — maybe centuries — for the rock edges where they entered were worn smooth, their droppings were everywhere and an unsavoury smell emanated from the cavity.

Randal scrambled up and placing his gun against the rock, peered into the fissure. It was just large enough for a man to crawl through, but all was darkness — a blackness intensified by the brilliance of the light outside.

How he wished he had brought his torch! Indeed, he had certainly intended doing so, but had overlooked it when packing that morning.

He rose to his feet and looked about him. There were no shrubs or trees at this level but where a little soil had built up between some stones, a clump of coarse reed-like grass had grown. He selected the longest he could find, a piece of perhaps four feet, and dropping to his knees, reached into the cavity, poking about in all directions with the grass stalk. His probing revealed some obstruction immediately ahead, but further exploration suggested an empty space to the right of it. The thought of having to return to his camp for the torch depressed him, so before doing so he decided to risk venturing in a little way further, and with the aid of the grass, at least satisfy himself as to whether the cavity was negotiable once the obstacle had been rounded.

Lowering himself onto his stomach, he crawled in and found that once through the opening, he had ample width and sufficient height to move on hands and knees. Feeling for the obstruction he eased himself around it and was surprised to see a glimmer of light in the distance. Closing his eyes for a few moments to accustom them to the darkness and groping about him, he discovered that it was now wide enough for comfort but that the roof was still too low to allow him to stand upright. He moved forward gingerly, feeling his way along the walls and roof as he progressed, but as his eyes became more used to the darkness and the strength of the distant light increased, he was able to advance more comfortably and was about to enter what turned out to be a fair-sized cavern, when he stopped suddenly.

He now recalled with some concern that the flat stone had been removed from the entrance. Surely if someone had entered he would have replaced the stone on leaving! Was someone still inside? Until that moment he had not been concerned with being quiet but now he remained still for several minutes. Somewhere there was water dripping and the atmosphere instead of being arid as one would have expected was moist and clammy.

Randall moved forward — quietly now — and as he neared the mouth of the cave saw that the roof dropped sharply towards the cave floor so that the gap decreased to a slit of perhaps eighteen inches as it opened onto a narrow shelf on the hillside. From the ground this ledge would have obscured the cave entrance to some extent, suggesting it to be shallower than it was. This indeed, was how it had seemed to him on the previous day when he had watched the *dassies* sunning themselves on this eastern side of the hill, and then disappearing into the crevice when the eagle swooped at them.

Because of the sun's present position — it being almost midday — a shaft of light was directed through the opening which clearly revealed the immediate centre of the cave, but conversely, intensified the shadows at each side. He made his way towards the opening, intending to peer through before making any search of his surroundings. The foul stench that pervaded the air was overpowering, so that he was unable to control himself and his gorge rose. He vomited several times and for a while, leant against the wall to recover. A gleam of light was reflected from something in the dust of the floor. He leaned forward to examine it — a golden sovereign, another, then three or four more in close proximity. Many more were spilling from what looked to have once been a leather saddle bag, mostly rotten or eaten away. As he stooped, his eye was caught by something in the shadow. A boot. Two boots — and in the boots were feet, with legs and above that a body! A rotting, stinking, putrid, maggot-infested corpse!

Revulsion overcame him and he disgorged again, then on all fours crept to the opening, where, putting his head through, he gulped lungfuls of the clean, sweet, pure, wonderful air.

It was a full fifteen minutes before he felt able to return and look once more upon the corpse. The humid heat, blowflies and possibly small animals and ants, had rendered the body unrecognizable. In many places where the clothes were not holding it together, the bones and joints were exposed. The body had been clothed in a red and black chequered shirt, khaki shorts and a green army fatigue cap lay nearby — clothes that Welch had been reported as wearing when he had set out on his 'prospecting' trip. Rodents had nibbled through one of the large buttoned pockets of the shirt, exposing what appeared to be a pocket-book.

Sickened, Randall forced himself to undo the button and withdrew the articles — a slim wallet and a passport. He carried the latter to the light and flicked open the pages and if any confirmation had been needed, page one provided it. Name of bearer — Allen Welch.

Surely a passport was a curious item to take with him on an expedition into the bush? Not so strange perhaps if his intention had been to leave the country quietly, immediately after completing his project. A project he must have felt reasonably confident of carrying through successfully.

It was only now that he realized he should not have handled the articles, and the police would be sure to criticize him for doing so, but it could be of no real consequence, for he had not been in the district when the man had died and there would be no difficulty in proving this. Another point in his favour was his having discussed with both Sturman and Steyn, his deciphering of the message from the old book. He would hardly have done that if there were anything to hide. On the contrary, they would surely appreciate that, without his help, they may well have never known of Welch's death at all. He might have lain here undiscovered for years — generations even.

Now he perceived how Welch had died. The body was slumped against a large boulder to one side of the opening. The rusty blade of an old stabbing spear had penetrated his throat, the tip of which was still protruding through the back of his neck, and as he died, his right hand had clutched at the haft, just below the blade, in a futile effort to extract it. A small automatic lay where he must have dropped it as he grabbed at the spear that was tearing out his life. His left arm must have been thrown up before him in a vain endeavour to ward off the blow, for the sleeve and flesh of this arm had been ripped bare, exposing the bone from wrist to elbow.

What had actually happened on that fateful day when both Kabatenga and Welch had met their deaths, could only be conjecture. Welch had probably hoped to find the coins' hiding-place on his own, but was quite prepared to use force on Kabatenga to reveal it if necessary. Knowing that the presence of a strange white-man in the area would soon reach the man's ears, he had lain in wait. At last his patience had been rewarded. Kabatenga, perhaps anxious to know whether the hoard had been discovered by the so-called prospector in the area, had let his concern overcome his caution — had visited the *dassie* passage cavern and been followed into it by Welch. Kabatenga could have heard him and taken up the old spear that had been there for decades — may well have known of its presence there.

Welch, with his automatic, would have felt that he had nothing to fear from an unarmed man, and approaching from the darkness would have an additional advantage; to the African he would have been hardly discernible. Welch may well have fired a shot at him. In his terror, Kabatenga had probably eased himself through the cave opening and onto the narrow ledge, taking the old spear with him. Welch, still believing him to be unarmed, had approached the opening — might even have fired again (though obviously he had not hit Kabatenga, for no gunshot wounds had been found on him). The African in his panic, had thrust the spear wildly through the opening in the white man's direction and it had found its mark, but this had never been known to him, for in his terror, he had slipped from the ledge, to crash some eighty feet below, suffering the terrible injuries that Changa had described.

★ ★ ★

The *dassies* were now apparently transferring again from one side of the hill to the other, for Randall could hear the slight sounds they were making as they scrambled over the loose surface of the passage behind him.

He smiled to himself. They were naturally very timid and would be in for a big surprise when they found him occupying the cave.

Curious to know if any shots had, in fact, been fired by Welch, he picked up the automatic and held it out in front of him, the better to examine it in the brighter light, and again heard the *dassies*.

A shot rang out and reverberated around the cavern.

Pellets spattered the wall to his left. A searing pain burned the fingers which held the automatic, causing him to drop it. He threw himself against the wall, into the shadow, in an effort to make himself less conspicuous.

Whoever had followed him had brought his, Randall's double-barrelled .410 with him. There was a second charge that might at any moment tear into his body. The gun had been loaded with bird-shot in both barrels but a clean hit at that close range could be the end of him. Only the fact that he had been holding his hand extended before him, and his assailant's obviously poor aim had saved him from being seriously wounded by that first shot.

He was scared to death. This was not the ending he had envisaged when setting out on what he anticipated would be an enjoyable excursion. Steyn had warned him not to meddle — to pack it up. It was too late now. Any second burning lead might crash into him.

Terrified, he groped in the dust with his left hand and his fingers closed over the automatic. How many cartridges had it originally been loaded with? How many, if any, had been fired by Welch? Was the barrel filled with sand? Was it jammed? Would it fire?

Randal wasn't naturally left-handed. Didn't know if the gun's safety-catch was off, or even if it had a safety-catch. He pointed it in the direction from which the shot had come and pressed the trigger — again, again and again. One, two, three, four shots rang out and the 'ping' of the bullets as they ricocheted from the rocky sides echoed round the cave.

An agonized cry rang out — then a sobbing, followed by a desperate plea. 'Don't shoot. You've hit me. I'm bleeding.'

The voice was that of a European.

For some moments there was silence. Randall felt weak with relief. He had pressed the trigger several times after the fourth shot and realized the automatic was then empty. Even as he squatted there in the shadow it dawned on him that it had not been the *dassies* that he had heard. They would not have been coming from the direction of the passage — being morning they would have been on this side of the hill sunning themselves outside. He would have given a lot to be doing the same.

There was still the cartridge in the man's gun and that cry might just be a trap to get him to make a false move. Should he trust this person? That pathetic cry had seemed genuine — of that he felt certain.

★  ★  ★

Apart from the intermittent drip of water the cavern was in silence again. He heard a stone move. Perhaps even now the wounded man was taking up a position the better to fire on him. A minute later and the silence was again broken by renewed and frightened sobs coming from the darkness.

Randall's voice was hoarse. 'You there,' he called and clearing his throat began again. 'You there. If you don't want to get another bullet, put your gun on the floor with the butt towards me, and on your hands and knees push it slowly in front of you.'

A shuffling movement indicated that his order was being complied with and he soon saw the butt of the gun moving steadily in his direction. Unarmed as he was, it was a great relief to know that the other was obeying his instructions. His right hand was smarting painfully and he could feel the blood dripping from the tips of his fingers. Until then these had been numb, but now he flexed them and

169

realized with relief that no bones had been broken.

A few yards away the crawling man came into sight, pushing the weapon before him with one hand, the other being clutched to his body. Changing the automatic to his injured right hand and pointing it menacingly at his adversary, Randall stretched forward with his left and withdrew the shotgun from the other's grasp.

The wounded man presented a pitiful sight, for apart from a blood-soaked left arm, he was obviously utterly exhausted and very frightened.

In spite of his own harrowing experience — or indeed perhaps from an overwhelming sense of relief — Randall now felt only sympathy for the wretch — someone whom he need no longer fear.

They stared at one another for some moments, neither knowing how to broach an introduction, until Randall, observing that the other was on the point of fainting, broke the silence.

'Come over to the light near the

entrance and let's have a look at that arm of yours.'

As they moved forward, towards the stronger light at the cave's narrow opening, the newcomer suddenly became aware of the repulsive object that had once been the living Welch. He was overcome and became sick, but vomited little, his stomach seemingly being empty.

Randall also retched again, then hastily tore open the man's shirt sleeve. As far as he could make out in the uncertain light, the wound did not look serious. There was no sign of the slug. Either it had ploughed through surface flesh or a flying piece of stone, smashed by a misdirected bullet, had caused the wound which was by this time bleeding only slightly.

It was now essential to get out of the foul tomb before the unwholesome environment infected their injuries. He bound the other's arm with his handkerchief, replaced the automatic close to the body where he had found it, and placing a single sovereign in his pocket indicated his intention of leaving.

'Look, I didn't come intending to kill

you . . . ' The stranger started to explain.

'Skip the explanations,' Randall interrupted him. Let's get out of here,' and feeling assured that he would not now be attacked, led the way.

Getting out was going to be more difficult than getting in, for then they had the glimmer of light in the distance, once they had rounded the obstacle near the entrance, whereas on the return they would be looking into darkness until almost out.

Feeling their way gingerly, they started off standing upright, then as the roof lowered, resorted to all fours and eventually, after skirting the bulge of rock, the opening to the daylight was before them, and one behind the other they squeezed themselves through it.

No sooner were they out, than the second man again attempted to explain himself.

'I'm Thomson. I watched you disappear into this opening and . . . '

Once more he was interrupted. 'When we get down and have rested and I have had a thorough look at your arm and my hand we will have much to discuss. In the meantime conserve your strength, for by the look of you, you are going to need it,' Randall instructed him.

The sun was by this time almost overhead and to their eyes, accustomed to darkness, the glare was blinding.

A blue-headed lizard, basking on a rock, stared at them momentarily as if doubting its senses at seeing two humans emanating from the bowels of the hill, then darted for safety down a crevice.

Now in the open he regarded his erstwhile potential killer with interest. Above average in height, but decidedly underweight, his features were sharp, the facial bones pronounced — excessively pronounced he thought. From what cause he wondered? Illness? Lack of food?

His age? Difficult to estimate. Late thirties perhaps. His hair showed no sign of greying. His moustache had not been trimmed recently nor had the rest of his face seen a razor for some days. The grey-blue eyes though deep-set and tired-looking were kindly and his voice had been pleasant. His hands long and

173

slender were not those of an artisan's — more likely an artist's or a musician's.

In spite of having been so nearly killed by this gaunt and haggard man, Randall now felt only compassion for him. He slung his .410 across his back.

'You climb down to the cave first,' he told Thomson, and found it necessary to give the man a certain amount of assistance, for apart from his being less robust than himself, the wounded arm was putting him at a considerable disadvantage.

Scrambling down he joined the other at the entrance to the large cave, picked up his rucksack and looked about him with a view to finding a suitable spot to rest, make tea and share what little sustenance he had in his bag. It was his intention to spend the night there also, for a good night's rest in addition to food and drink, was a vital necessity for Thomson, if he were not to become seriously ill.

Imparting this intention to Thomson, the latter, to Randall's surprise, pointed out a small area some fifty yards away to their left, and a little lower down the hill, which levelled off there most conveniently. They made their way towards it and Randall was especially pleased to find that at this place a rocky prominence jutted outwards, creating a small patch of shade — a shade most welcome, for the heat now being reflected from the granite boulders was intense and sapped their depleted strength.

Randall unpacked his bag. There was little enough for two — something less than a quart of water, some tea, sugar, a very small tin of pressed beef and a few oatmeal biscuits.

Thomson seated himself wearily upon a convenient root which grew from the rock base and leaning his back against the rock wall, closed his eyes.

Randall busied himself with making a fire and very quickly had the water boiling. He allowed the tea to brew before arousing his companion, and handed him a mugful, which he had sweetened liberally, then opened the can of meat. He ate sparingly himself, merely sufficient to avoid embarrassment to his companion by not doing so.

Once Thomson had emptied his mug, Randall took a little himself, but again ensured that enough for another full mug remained, and only after the stranger had finished this too, did he question him concerning his involvement.

# 14

'Did you know Welch, the corpse in the cave?' Randall asked.

'Only slightly,' Thomson told him. 'He left the mine at about the same time as Burnett. I didn't know either of them very well but from what I saw, it seemed to me that they had known one another prior to coming to the mine, and Welch is — or rather was — the only person I can think of, apart from myself, who might have got an inkling of what Burnett was really after.

'They had been room-mates in the single quarters when Burnett had had that dose of blackwater fever. Perhaps they had been on the search together, but I don't think so. Burnett was a taciturn man and I doubt if he would have given away anything voluntarily, especially if it had to do with money.

'It is more likely that Welch had thought things out for himself from careless remarks he had heard. Fancy the poor blighter ending up like that, with a spear through his neck!'

He drained a few more drops of tea from the mug and continued.

'How long do you think he has been dead?'

Randall shifted his position slightly to escape the glare from the sun which had cleared the rock edge and was now directly in his eyes.

'About four or five weeks I should say,' he replied. 'But tell me now, how did you get involved in this business and why did you try to kill me?'

'I had to. It was you or me, wasn't it? I'll start at the beginning. As I told you, my name is Thomson, Arnold Thomson. I had been Burnett's ward-mate in the small Lucy's Luck mine hospital and knew him of course, as we were both employed at the mine. Burnett, Welch and myself being single, took our meals at the mine boarding-house. Welch was always a free talker and some time after Burnett's illness he hinted that Burnett was interested in something big, apart from the spare-time working of his Mamba's Hole mine.

'Reflecting on this, I thought back to the way he had behaved while we were in hospital together. He had been terribly ill with blackwater fever — I certainly had not expected him to recover — and he had rambled incoherently for most of the first night. At that time I had not concerned myself with his ramblings, just hoping that he would be quiet and let me get some sleep. It was only later, when considering the other incidents, that I recalled that he had mentioned the word 'cave' more than once.'

He flicked his hand at a butterfly which, attracted by the moist sweat that streamed from his forehead, was hovering about his face.

Wiping away the sweat he too moved further back to escape the sun.

'You mentioned 'other incidents',' Randall prompted him.

'Yes,' Thomson continued. 'He had been anxious for the ward-sister to fetch a book from his quarters, which she eventually did. He had dozed off meanwhile, and I, having nothing to read just then, took up the book and skimmed through it. It was a very short work — a biography. When he awoke and saw me with it he was most annoyed. Later he dropped a sovereign which I retrieved for him, and I passed some light-hearted remark about it. He was furious with me, accusing me of interfering. At the time, I put his manner down to his illness, but later came to the conclusion that Welch was right, and Burnett had indeed become interested in something more lucrative than prospecting. As I have said, I read the book only cursorily, but connecting it as I did with the sovereign he had dropped — and I had noticed that it was a Queen Victoria coin, in excellent condition — I felt reasonably sure that I knew what he was after and that it was in some way connected with the 'cave' he had mumbled about.

'I had no means of knowing where he had obtained the sovereign or in which of the hundreds of granite hills throughout Rhodesia the supposed cave was situated so put the matter from my mind.

'After hearing of the finding of Burnett's body I recalled that his boss-boy, Gideon, had died in an accident a little while before the estimated time of his own demise and I became suspicious that the two deaths might have been connected, so one Saturday afternoon I went over to the Mamba's Hole and made a few enquiries, including an interview with his, Gideon's widow. I got the impression that she too had felt that his death had not been accidental but had somehow been contrived. I reasoned then, that supposing Burnett had engineered Gideon's death (and I must admit I couldn't see how), it must have been either to keep him quiet about something or else get him out of the way.

'I told the widow that Burnett had had a sovereign and asked her if she had any idea how he might have acquired it. She seemed rather reluctant to say anything about that, but although I hadn't said so, I think she presumed I was a detective and did admit that her late husband had given it to Burnett, but did not explain why. I reasoned that it was to encash for him. It followed, or so I reckoned, that the boss-boy was the most likely lead to any hoard. So I then asked her what tribal district he came from. She told me it was Changa's village, in the Bamatuzi Tribal Trust area. I knew roughly where that was. I am a draughtsman by profession and had previously worked in the government survey department.

'I now made up my mind to do a spot of 'prospecting' for myself — for ready minted gold!

'With Burnett dead, I considered that there was no urgency. Whoever had discovered the cache was apparently not spending it fast, or news of it would have spread. I did not want to lose my job by going off without notice on a wild-goose chase and so applied for a fortnight's leave. I still had no idea in which hill the cave might be, but camped out on Crown land near Changa's village, pretending that I was doing a little prospecting. For five or six days I searched from dawn to dusk for any likely cave but it seemed hopeless. I did find several small caves, one of which, on that hill over there, has some beautifully preserved Bushman paintings on the walls, but there was never a sign of what I was looking for.

'Then, about a week ago, I met three natives at a stream crossing. They were hunting with dogs and at first showed considerable suspicion of me, especially as I had no servant, but after I had given them some tobacco and sugar (this latter I could ill afford), they explained their reasons for being so suspicious. Except for the routine visit of the District Commissioner and occasionally a police trooper, they seldom saw a white-man in that area. Now there had been two of us within a short period, both professing to be prospectors and neither of us having native carriers.

'Some days after the arrival of that other prospector, a man of their village, Kabatenga by name, had been killed in a very mysterious manner (and judging by their attitude they had obviously regarded him with some awe). Coincidentally or otherwise, the white man had not been seen since. I asked them to describe this man. They told me of his stocky build and dark hair and described his clothing, which agrees with that found on Welch's corpse. I had no idea then that Welch had any interest in the sovereigns, though I do now recall his having left the mine about the same time Burnett did. I recognized the name Kabatenga as being the totem name of the deceased Gideon, for his wife had casually mentioned it. My spirits which had slumped considerably with my weariness chirped up somewhat. Perhaps after all the searching, I had at last received a positive clue. 'Where had Kabatenga died?' I asked them. Perhaps unconsciously and unwisely, I had shown a certain excitement, for they closed up like clams and even the promise of additional tobacco would not loosen their tongues. They did not know where he died — not one of them. Quite happy before to while away their time in talking, they now conveniently realized that they had a long way to go in a short time, and left hurriedly.

'My excitement turned to depression. I had spent all that time in fruitless searching and now it seemed that the mysterious stranger may well have found what he had come searching for, even if, as it appeared, he had had to murder for it. Nevertheless, I spent a further few days scouring the district, still hoping that the other man had been unsuccessful. The African's death could have been an accident and have had no connection in any way with the other white prospector.

'I was now very depressed, already feeling unwell from exhaustion and lack of proper and sufficient food and made up my mind to return, when yesterday I saw the dust your car was making in the sandy track going towards Changa's village. Police, I wondered? I was not above a mile and a half away when I saw you enter the village. I guardedly approached and noticed that you were not in uniform and also that your car was not an official one, so even your being from the C.I.D. seemed unlikely. I crept up fairly close and with my binoculars, studied you carefully, but I had never seen you before.

'There was now only one day's leave left to me but I decided to wait awhile and see what you were up to. I had been sleeping wherever night caught me, only returning to my camp when necessary, so had my sleeping bag and a little food with me. I watched you talking to the headman and when you left with a youth, I tailed you until you reached the base of the other side of this hill. Judging by your careful examination of the spot I concluded, rightly, as it now appears, that that was where the African had died. The youth had now left you and for a long time I watched you closely examining the face of the hill with your glasses. When you came around to this side of the hill I followed you again. I could sense that you knew where you were making for. I watched as you scanned this hill from the smaller one and saw you climb up to the large cave and enter it, and when you returned I quite expected to see you carrying some container heavy with sovereigns. I have no idea what I would have done. I was near the end of my tether, tired, weak and mentally exhausted. Completely unarmed I would have been quite incapable of overpowering you, even if it had occurred to me.

'To my surprise, you left the cave with nothing more than with what you entered. It was near evening and I last saw you striding off in the direction of your camp.

'Once you were out of sight I scrambled to the cave as best I could and realized as soon as I entered it, that nothing could have been hidden there that would not have been quickly discovered. I left the cave and descended the hill to this level, but was some thirty yards further over there to our left. You see that large group of rocks? Well, amongst them is a small flat area covered in light brushwood and grass. I made my way there, cleared a small patch in the centre, made a fire, brewed the last of my tea, and partly roasted a potato in the embers, which was all the food I had left. I say partly roasted, because I was so dead beat I could not wait for it to be completely cooked. I managed to eat a little and not feeling up to collecting grass for bedding, crept exhausted into my sleeping-bag.

'I was unable to sleep, except very fitfully, until well into the early hours and was surprised to find when I did awake, that the sun was high — the bushes amongst which I had bedded down and the fact that I was on the shady side of the hill, had kept the early sunlight from me as I slept. There was no more food or tea, only a little sweetened condensed milk so I heated up some water and added that.

'A soon as I had drunk, I prepared to leave and was just wondering whether I should try to reach my camp and car (which attempt, I feared might have meant my ending up as Burnett had done), or whether to go to Changa's village which is nearer, when I heard some pebbles trickling down the hillside.

'Peering surreptitiously through the bushes, I saw that it was you who were once again making your way up to the cave. I was certainly surprised, knowing that you had spent so long searching there yesterday. I watched you push through the bushes to the left of the cave and saw you reach the ledge above it.

'You disappeared suddenly and when you had not emerged after a few minutes, I followed furtively after you and somehow managed to reach the ledge, and of course noticed the hole through which you had obviously entered and saw your gun against the rock. I don't know what I had in mind to do. I certainly had no definite intention of killing you. Perhaps I thought to threaten you — to demand a portion of your find if you had been successful, in return for my keeping silent.

'Beyond logical reasoning and thoroughly scared at the prospect of entering that black hole, I did so, and dragging the gun with me moved stealthily forward. Round the bend I could see the light and a little further on could see the cavern. As I neared it, I saw you lift the bag and coins spill out, but could not see what else you were doing. You seemed to be examining something in the light, then suddenly I realized that you had an automatic in your hand which you raised and pointed in my direction. I felt sure that you were about to kill me.

'Without aiming, and from my crouching position, I fired. You fired back several times and I called out. I thought that I had been seriously wounded.'

Randall considered the ill, weak and frightened man.

'I had no idea that there was anyone else in the passage and it was sheer coincidence that I appeared to be pointing it at you. I was holding it in the light to try to find out if in fact Welch had fired it. I had actually heard a slight movement just before you fired, but I thought that it was being made by some *dassies*. I hadn't the slightest fear of anyone having followed me, for, as far as I was aware, the only persons who might have been interested were all dead.

'Well now, as I said before, I think it will be best if we spend the night here. You have been badly knocked up and I think that another few miles walk would not improve matters. It's comfortable here and your arm doesn't seem to be worrying you too much. I've some antiseptic in my car and we need some food and I, my blankets, so I'll go and fetch them right away. There's a sledge track going from Changa's right down the *vlei* to close to where Kabatenga was found, and I think I will be able to drive down it if I'm careful. In fact, except for an anthill here and there I shouldn't have much trouble in getting right down to the base of this hill — possibly to within a quarter of a mile of here.

'Allowing an hour's walk to my camp and twenty minutes to load up, I should be back here in under two hours, providing I don't have any mishaps. We will camp here for the night then, and leave for Bulawayo tomorrow.'

'What about the money?' Thomson tentatively asked him. 'Surely you are not going to leave it — after all, we two are the only ones who know that there is such a hoard?'

Thomson may have been very weak and far from well, but the thought of maybe, even a small share in all that wealth perked up his spirits considerably.

That suggestion of a share-out was not

what Randall had in mind and he quickly let the other man know what action he intended taking.

'It will be a matter for the government to decide and though we seem to have reached the same conclusion as to its source, it is unlikely that it will ever be proved and so I expect it will be declared 'treasure trove' and I hope will be adjudged to me, as finder. What is certain, is that we cannot just take it and say nothing about Welch's death there. Mind you, as the hoard has been found on Tribal Trust land, that may rule out our getting anything at all.'

Thomson noted the use of the word 'our' in Randall's last remark with considerable relief, but made no further comment.

Randall rose and taking his gun prepared to depart.

'Right. I'll be off then. See you in a couple of hours.'

# 15

The thought that in his absence Thomson might rob the cave of its cache did not enter Randall's head, nor indeed need he have been concerned if it had crossed his mind. Thomson was now too weak to climb to the entrance, and to have entered that dark passage again and confront the corpse was something that he would never do on his own account for any amount.

So Randall set off for the camp. He too was now feeling the strain. His right hand throbbed painfully and the movement of walking aggravated it. He slung his gun onto his back and slipped the painful hand inside his shirt as a sling.

It was now early afternoon but the heat was still oppressive and waves of nausea periodically came over him.

A grey lourie bird called out, 'go away, go away' monotonously, and with almost human mimicry.

Normally a keen naturalist who enjoyed the calls of the bush, this command now irritated him intensely.

The bird was perched near the top of a nearby euphorbia tree, and again screeched its nasal demand for him to be gone.

He unslung his .410 and though the exasperating bird was well out of range he fired off a shot in its general direction, startling a pair of francolins which rose with raucous squawks almost at his feet. The 'go-away' bird in the meantime departed to a more distant tree where it was joined by a second, both of which voiced their disapproval.

Back on the hill, Thomson, having heard the shot, imagined all sorts of calamities to have befallen Randall. Had he been bitten by a snake and fired to kill the reptile? Perhaps hurt himself and fired the gun to attract assistance? He remained in a state of nervous apprehension all the time his companion was away.

Randall pushed on towards his camp near the village, following the sledge track, which though necessitating a longer journey, provided the opportunity to examine the route he intended to take when returning by car later.

He thought back over the events of the past week. It was exactly a week ago that he had attended the auction sale and it seemed incredible that so much had happened to him in such a short time. He would have some things to say to Sturman if he ever met him again. That man had ridiculed his suggestion that there might have been some connection between what Welch had playfully put into code in the old book, and Burnett's death. Steyn, he thought, had taken it more seriously, though even he had not openly shown any interest.

How had it all come about? One could only surmise, but from the evidence it seemed that Burnett had come to the conclusion that Gideon's brother, Kabatenga, had found a hidden cache of sovereigns somewhere in the Bamatuzi Trust area, and apparently in a cave — for Thomson had heard him mention the word 'cave' when he was in hospital with him.

Burnett, instead of coming straight to this district, had thought to hide his intentions by going out on the Victoria Falls road and then cutting across to the native reserve from the opposite direction — a journey of several days. How Welch knew where he was likely to be at the exact time was a mystery, but he certainly seemed to have tracked Burnett down and somehow contrived his death before making his own way back to this area.

Unfortunately for Welch however, he had dropped his watch at the scene.

Steyn had not deemed the finding of the watch as being of any importance, offering several logical explanations for its being there.

Well, he, Randall had made Steyn change his mind before and both Steyn and Sturman had another surprise coming to them when he informed them of his new discoveries.

Randall still wondered how Welch had eventually come to realize the significance of the two words that he, Welch, had written in the back of his watch.

While musing on these matters Randall had made good progress and rounding a small hillock, his own car came into sight. His own car — and another! A small van with the police insignia plainly visible!

For a moment his heart jumped. What had he done that was illegal? Nothing that he could think of. This was the usual routine visit of the police to outlying districts in all probability, and finding his, Randall's camp, they were curious to know his business.

Though several hundred yards away, he had now been spotted and an officer had come to the edge of the clearing to await his arrival. An African constable stood near to the van. He recognized the officer as Sergeant Steyn — thanks be it wasn't Sturman, he thought.

'So! It's you,' was Steyn's opening remark. 'I thought as much. I asked you to keep out of this affair.'

'What affair?' Randall countered.

'You know what I am getting at,' he was told. 'Those two words in the watch. You have obviously discovered their implication. When you were in my office on

Wednesday I noticed that the African hesitated at those words and I realized that they meant something to him, in spite of his denial. I telephoned through to the Department of Native Affairs and asked them if those words had any meaning for them. They made a few enquiries, but neither were known to them but did point out that the word 'Endwatuge' might be intended for 'Ndwatuka', a hill reputed to be the residence of an oracle in the pre-European days and they told me where it was.

'I then telephoned through to the police post in this district and asked them if the word 'Kabatenga' had any significance. They informed me that it was the name of a family reputed to be connected with the oracle and that a man of that name had recently been killed after an apparent accidental fall from that particular hill and that some days before the occurrence a white prospector had left his car and some gear at a small native village some ten miles away from here. He had asked the villagers to keep their eye on them for a few days, but since then he had not returned and the natives feared for his safety.

'As a matter of interest, I also contacted a native police constable in the area in which Burnett died and he confirmed that a second white man had been seen in the district at about that time. There had seemed no connection as the two men had not been seen together.

'I have reason to believe that the missing man is Welch,' he continued. 'The thing is, where is he now?'

'I can tell you where he is,' Randall at last managed to get in his say. 'He's in a cave on that hill — a cave previously known only to the Kabatenga family.'

Steyn cut him short. 'Get in my van. Let's go. He may disappear.'

'He won't disappear,' the other told him. 'He's dead. Very! With a spear through his throat. There's no hurry.'

Randall suddenly felt spent, and a feeling of intense relief overcame him. Here was someone to take the responsibility off his hands. Thanks be it wasn't Sturman. That man would have irritated him — would have made him feel unco-operative. Just as well though, that he had not done as Thomson had suggested — just taken the gold and said nothing about Welch's death, for once having got onto the trail, Steyn would have doggedly persevered and then he could have found himself in a very awkward situation.

This reminded him that he had one of the coins in his pocket and considered it a propitious moment to mention it. He withdrew it and with a certain feeling of satisfaction, presented it to the officer.

'This is what they were after,' he told him. 'I should think there must be several hundreds of them up there in the cave, and at today's price their value might well exceed ten thousand pounds.'

'I suppose you have already formed an opinion as to the original source of the coins,' Steyn suggested, amicably enough, but without completely veiling a hint of sarcasm.

Thankful as he was to have someone to relieve him from further responsibility, Randall could not resist keeping to himself, for just a little longer, the fact that he really was in a position to suggest a logical explanation.

'I think so. Yes,' he answered.

Steyn's eyebrows lifted in undoubted surprise. 'And the source is?' he asked.

'Well it is only my theory,' Randall told him, 'but everything points to its being the correct one. It certainly was not Lobengula's treasure — if there ever was one. The spot where he was reputed to have buried it is miles from here.

'Have you read any of the history relating to the Matabele War and the flight and pursuit of the old king?'

'Naturally,' Steyn acknowledged. 'No Rhodesian — born or immigrant — will ever forget the heroic 'last stand' and total annihilation of the Allan Wilson Patrol.'

Randall nodded in agreement. 'Well, that massacre might never have happened. You will recall how Lobengula, ill and hard-pressed, was anxious to reach a peaceful settlement with the whites and sent an emissary with a petition to the Rhodesian commander, and as an earnest of his good faith, tendered a bag of money. The first white men the messenger met were two troopers who had become separated from the main company. He handed over the money to them and delivering his appeal, the messenger returned to the retreating king's retinue.

'Whether or not the troopers understood the message, they certainly did not pass it on, and stole the offering. The duplicity was later discovered and they were tried and convicted, but no trace of the money was ever found. That you will know is not fiction, but recorded fact.

'I think that Burnett, Thomson (whom you have not met), and myself, all came to the same conclusion — that the sovereigns were part of the king's peace-offering. All three of us had seen a short biography of a young man who had himself been active in the Matabele War and who had given a more detailed account of the handing over of the payment to the troopers and suggesting that it was generally presumed that they had hidden it immediately.

'We know that Lobengula was paid one hundred sovereigns per month by the

British South Africa Company for mineral rights, so he certainly had sovereigns to offer and they were of course the legal tender at that time.

'It does seem likely that the two troopers hid the money as the biography had suggested, but not I think, in that place, for it would have been discovered by Kabatenga's grandfather and he would surely have moved it, reasoning that whoever had hidden it would return for it some day. It is more likely that the grandfather saw the troopers hide the hoard somewhere and subsequently moved it to the cave, knowing that only his family would have dared to climb the venerated hill. I have learned that Kabatenga's father did not practise as an *nganga* so may never have entered the cavern himself. Whether this was so or not, I think it unlikely that Kabatenga ever heard about it for his father died when he was a child.

'Because of his family ancestry though, he would not have any dread of the hill and perhaps from curiosity regarding his forbear's association with the oracle there, had freely roamed the hillside and probably only quite recently had discovered the entrance to the hiding-place. I can't see there being any claimants but myself,' he added hopefully.

Steyn had listened attentively to Randall's theory.

'Yours sounds a reasonable explanation,' he said, 'but who is entitled to what you have found, will be for the authorities to decide.'

After imparting the information, Randall had quickly collected his few goods and stowed them in his vehicle.

'Who is this chap Thomson you mentioned, and where does he come into it?' Steyn asked.

'It's a long story which I will tell you later. I have left him near the cave. He is very knocked up and has a badly cut arm. I promised him I would return as quickly as I could, so let's be on our way. I've checked the route and I think that with a bit of care, we can get the cars through to the other side of the hill.'

Steyn had not unloaded his own van while waiting at Randall's camp and so was also ready to move off. Before entering it he stopped, and regarding Randall purposefully, pointed to the latter's bloodstained hand.

'I suppose your own hand wouldn't be connected with that of your associate Thomson?' he hinted suspiciously.

'Well, you could say it was an accident in which we were both involved,' Randall agreed, making light of it.

Nevertheless he shivered slightly as he recalled how close to death he had felt when expecting that second shot which had not come, but he offered no further explanation to Steyn.

With Randall leading the way and choosing his route carefully, they set off, and with only a slight dent in the police van's fender when it brushed a tree stump while avoiding a hole, they were able to drive to within 500 yards of the base of the hill, then, carrying what items each would need for the night, they very soon reached the clearing where Thomson was waiting.

At the sight of the police officer the apprehensive Thomson withdrew into his shell, fearing that Randall had, after all, laid a charge against him.

Randall introduced the two men and gave a quick and rough explanation as to how Thomson had become involved and how each had come by their wounds.

It was now past three o'clock and the sun had cleared the overhanging rock, in the welcome shade of which the two men had bivouacked after leaving the cave. The fire was rekindled, water soon boiling, and tea made. Steyn and the African constable had had no drink since late morning. Thomson too, though somewhat recovered from his earlier low state was still far from fit and needed the brandy with which Steyn had liberally laced his cup. The officer had also brought a small first-aid kit from the police van and dressed the wounds of both men.

Thomson, no doubt cheered by the brandy, and relieved that his arm was not seriously wounded became quite voluble, talking freely with Steyn about the persons involved and their relationships with each other when working on the mine.

Randall's thoughts wandered. Ever since they had left the cave some three hours earlier, something had been nagging at his mind. Was it something in the cave he had seen, or should have seen — or perhaps had actually seen, but which he had failed to interpret correctly? Goodness knows, he had not spent a minute longer in there than he needed to, and if it had not been for the delay occasioned by Thomson's shooting at him, he would not have spent more than a few minutes in that stinking sepulchre, so could not blame himself if he had overlooked something.

Almost as soon as he had found Welch and the sovereigns his thoughts had been on saving his own life and then on caring for Thomson.

But there was something that he had missed. Of that he was becoming convinced.

He pictured himself back in the cave, starting from when he had first entered, and retraced in his mind every moment until they had left it.

In the background, he vaguely followed

the gist of the discussion going on.

He heard the name Westlake mentioned by Thomson and remembered how, at the Lucy's Luck, he had talked with Westlake himself — a decent fellow, and as it turned out, hailing from Randall's own hometown in England. He had discussed both Burnett and Welch with him. Surely something that Westlake had said had some relevance. But it would not come to mind.

How is it, that so often one is on the point of remembering something — knows one is on the point of it, and yet it remains just out of reach? The best thing is to try to recall incidents leading up to the problem. Better still, re-enact the incidents if possible.

He had come to a decision. Go back to the cave. It was the only thing to do.

# 16

He interrupted the other two. 'Sergeant Steyn, I can't help feeling that I missed something when in the cave this morning and won't feel happy until I have had another look. How do you feel about it?'

Steyn rose immediately. 'I was going to suggest that myself but thought you would turn it down, feeling that you had had enough for today. I know I could have insisted that you show me where it is — I presume that it is not in that large cave over to our right? But you found it and I thought I would let you show it to me when you felt ready to do so. Come.'

He rummaged in his case and brought out a large torch.

This time Randall was not to be caught out and had remembered to transfer his own torch from the car's pocket to his rucksack.

'It's going to be dark in there now, with no sun coming in from the far side, and the air is foul I can tell you,' he said, and prepared to move. 'I don't know if it will be any help, but I'm going to put this wet handkerchief over my nose and mouth. I was violently sick before and I expect I may be again. I'm not staying in there for more than a few minutes.'

Steyn wet his own handkerchief and followed. 'I don't intend to spend much time in there myself at the moment for there is nothing we can do this evening. C.I.D. bods will have to rig up lights and make a thorough search and get the body out. I hope they don't delay it long, it is going to be difficult enough as it is.'

Strong and fit, Steyn gave considerable help to Randall as he scaled the rock to the ledge where he was soon joined by the sergeant.

Randall eyed the narrow entrance and then the policeman's ample figure. Both he and Thomson, though slight, had had some difficulty in passing through the crevice and he now had some doubts as to whether Steyn would manage it.

The gap had sufficient height to pass through on one's stomach, but it was so narrow that his own shoulders had barely cleared it. Short of dynamite there was no possibility of widening the hole.

'Have we got to get through that?' Steyn asked.

'We have,' Randall told him.

'I'll never make it,' Steyn groaned in disappointment.

'It will be a squeeze for you,' Randall acknowledged, 'but if you can get through the immediate opening, you will find that it widens quickly. I will go through first, turn around, shine the torch, and help you.'

Randall proceeded with his suggestion and when he faced the opening again asked Steyn to lie prone and wriggle in as far as he could.

Steyn was not going to give up easily. As soon as his shoulders seemed likely to wedge, he twisted partly onto his side having found that the opening curved upwards slightly at the centre, and by pushing with his feet and with Randall pulling on his arms, he was soon far enough in to turn, firstly on his stomach again, then onto his knees.

Now with the aid of their torches they had no difficulty in avoiding any obstacles and very soon could see the slit of light coming from the other end of the cave.

They moved on quickly, their wet handkerchiefs by now almost dry. There must have been some moisture where the intermittent drips collected, but neither thought to remoisten them with water from that un-wholesome atmosphere. The two paused momentarily and between the sound of the drips Steyn was heard to swallow more than once.

Randall too, was already regretting his decision to revisit the cave. Exhausted both physically and mentally he wanted to turn and rush back — out into the fresh air.

Averting his eyes from the corpse, he hurried forward to the cave mouth — explained to Steyn how Kabatenga had fallen to his death and pointed out to him the broken bag with the sovereigns, and taking a deep breath, went over to the corpse.

He stared at the face which he did not remember having looked at before, and was appalled at what he saw. The skull was showing through the skin and the eye sockets were empty. He saw again the terrible wound in the throat with the protruding spear. The stench was horrible. Once again he was sick. Steyn had now joined him. He was wiping his mouth with his handkerchief and had clearly been similarly affected. Randall lowered his eyes to the body. Glancing down at the torn arm where the spear had ripped the flesh from wrist to elbow he noticed the calloused excrescence on the bone, as though it had been badly fractured at some time.

This was what he had noticed and forgotten!!

Randall thought back to his meeting with Maidwell that day at the railway station. Maidwell had told him of both Burnett and Welch being keen Rugby players and how Welch had broken his arm twice and in consequence had had to give up the game. This ugly lump on the bone, exposed by the rip of the spear was the obvious result of that double fracture. Westlake at the Lucy's Luck had also confirmed that Burnett had given up playing Rugby before arriving there.

Burnett?

Of course! It was *Burnett*, not Welch who had broken his arm. This foetid rotten corpse was not Welch as the passport indicated.

It was Burnett!

Confused and shattered by the new discovery and what it suggested, his immediate urge was to escape from this terrible place.

Now barely articulate, he drew the sergeant's attention to the callouses on the corpse's arm and without stating his intention, stumbled and groped his way towards the passage exit.

Steyn was not long in following and they lost no time in rejoining Thomson and the African, having been away less than forty minutes in all.

They had not spoken since leaving the sepulchre. Steyn deep in thought, was obviously greatly affected by what he had seen — large men often being over sensitive — and Randall himself had been deeply concentrating on the riddle of the change in identities.

Steyn broke the silence. 'You're a persistent blighter. You seem to have proved that Gideon's death was murder, and solved the mystery of Kabatenga's death, and now I suppose you are going to suggest that Welch somehow killed Burnett before coming here?'

'No.' Randall explained. 'It was the other way round. Burnett killed Welch and then came here. The corpse in there is Burnett. The broken bones in his arm will prove it.

'This, I think, is the probable explanation of why Burnett had first gone to the spot where his supposed body had been found, and gone there by such a round-about route. From the comments that Welch had made to him, he feared that his erstwhile room-mate had formed a shrewd idea of what he was after, but only vaguely the location. He reasoned too, that Welch, knowing what he did, would probably put two and two together and decide that he, Burnett had murdered Gideon and would quite likely make these suspicions known to the

215

police unless Burnett co-operated with him. Rather than have that threat hanging over him, Burnett had decided to get rid of Welch.

'How to do that without there being any suspicion resting on him was the problem. The most successful way is always to get rid of the body completely. If in doing so, he could fake his own death also, he would be free from the fear that the Repton police might, on their own initiative, conclude that Gideon's death had been homicide.

'They had both played as scrum-halves in rugby, always the smallest players in the side. Usually stocky, one scrum-half is often much like another as regards height and build. In this case there were even closer resemblances. Both had very dark hair and I think you will find that neither had dental plates.

'For what he had in mind, any small differences shouldn't really matter. There would be no reason for any doubts and queries if his plan were successful. He must have known of that out of the way spot, far from any native village (possibly

216

from some earlier prospecting trip during the time he had lived in Bulawayo), and no doubt also knew of some water hole not too far away.

'He arranged with Welch to meet him there secretly, he Welch, coming from the other direction — told him perhaps, that he knew where there was a fortune for the taking and suggested that he should be prepared with passport etc. and his car, and that in return for some assistance and old friendship's sake, they would share it and both leave the country quietly. Had suggested that it might be better not to be seen together; asked him to leave his car where he did, then walk across country to meet him.

'Welch had kept his side of the bargain, and after meeting Burnett had been killed by the latter. A tap on the head with a piece of hardwood covered with a sock perhaps, and then smothering, would have left no sign of violence — not after a few weeks in the tropics and in the spot he had chosen. Burnett would not have anticipated anyone finding the body for months.

'He had made no arrangements with anyone to pick him up, so there would have been no organized search until some native from the mine, or a creditor concerned for his dues, had reported him as missing.

'It had been sheer luck that the men looking for wild bees' nests stumbled on the body as early as they did.

'After murdering Welch, he had changed clothes with those of the corpse, left his own rifle, signet ring etc. and empty water-bottle but had failed to notice that Welch's watch had fallen from his pocket into the grass.

'It had been found some yards from the body, but Burnett may have carried or dragged the body some distance to a less conspicuous spot. He had then walked to this area, and his intention had been to get the sovereigns, collect Welch's car (having already elicited from him exactly where he had left it), and with his, Welch's, passport quietly leave the country as Welch.'

'Why do you think he deemed it necessary to kill Gideon?' Steyn questioned.

'When drunk, Gideon must have talked about the sovereigns as having come from Kabatenga and mentioned the word Ndwatuka and the word 'cave', but he had been unable to find out from him to what those words referred before Gideon passed out. Once sober, no amount of prising had produced any further explanation or elaboration and eventually Burnett had become exasperated.

'When his boss-boy had intimated that he wanted to go back to his village for a holiday, he suddenly realized that by examining his *chitupa* he could at least ascertain his village and tribal district and would base his search on this information. He would have been surprised to learn from it that Gideon's totem name was Kabatenga — then realizing that he was a brother, or at least a close relative of the person who had found the coins, he decided to get Gideon out of the way with the faked accident so that he would be unable to warn his relative or inform on Burnett, if eventually, he were forced to take some illegal action.'

Steyn listened intently to his reasoning. This or something like it, was what must have occurred.

'It's a nasty business. I suppose it will mean an exhumation of Welch's remains for positive identification, even though we can be sure that the body in the cave is that of Burnett. Dental charts of Welch will probably be the only positive proof we will be able to get at this late stage.'

Randall nodded in agreement. 'There is one small point that has just occurred to me,' he said. 'I think you will find that Burnett took a larger size in footwear than did Welch.'

'What gives you that idea?' the sergeant asked.

'Well, I don't know if you noticed it, but Burnett was wearing a good type of walking boot, yet Westlake told me that Welch always wore a suède type of *veldschoen* shoe. Burnett had been so careful with regard to his switch of identities that I cannot imagine him having overlooked the necessity to change his boots for Welch's shoes. I think he tried Welch's and found them too small for him. Had they been too large, no doubt he would have made do with them and squeezed his own onto the dead man's feet, but he just couldn't face that long walk with shoes too small for him and had to take that little risk.'

Steyn poured himself another mug of water. 'I think you've got something there. I seem to remember that the corpse that Inspector Sturman and I collected was wearing *veldschoens*, as you have suggested.'

Randall could be excused a certain smugness — it was only natural. Without his probing there could be little doubt that the truth might never have come to light. The sovereigns and the corpse could have remained undisturbed for a decade — a generation even.

No local natives would have climbed that hill because of their superstitions, and to any European who might have chanced on the small opening, it would have seemed of no importance — a hole for *dassies* to escape into.

★   ★   ★

The four now set about preparing a meal and arranging their sleeping positions. They had agreed to turn in early and make a day-break start on their return to Bulawayo.

# 17

The burning heat of the (so-called) suicide month — October — had come and gone. 'The 'rainbirds' (black and white cuckoos) had arrived and though the thunder-clouds were collecting every evening, heralding the approach of the first rains, they held off tantalizingly.

Two months had passed since Randall's discovery of the cave before he attended the magistrate's court to hear the government's ruling as to the ownership of the sovereigns.

Both Randall and Thomson had previously received summonses for their unauthorized presence in a native reserve, the former being additionally charged with hunting in that area, by virtue of his taking his gun with him.

They had both pleaded innocence, in that they did not realize that they were in a reserve, and that they had not been bent on any criminal activity.

Having heard the complete story from Sergeant Steyn, who stressed the invaluable help that Randall had given the authorities, and bearing in mind that the hill, Ndwatuka, was in fact, only just inside the reserve, the magistrate had merely given them a warning.

Now the day had arrived for the arbitrator's decision.

Briefly the magistrate summarized the cases presented by the various claimants.

The African Affairs Department had made claim on the grounds that it was 'treasure trove' found in a native reserve. Some of Kabatenga's relatives claimed that he had been the first to find it and it should be theirs. Changa maintained that being the village headman in whose 'custody' the sacred hill lay (but omitting to report that he himself would not dare set a foot on it), submitted his bid for entitlement.

Burnett's brother, in Australia, having read the full report in the cutting from the Rhodesian newspaper (considerately sent to him by the police, with the dead